Daughter of Son-Light

MW01681539

Daughter of Son-Light

Janet Leigh Kangas

Elisabeth S. McFadden

Pacific Press Publishing Association
Boise, Idaho
Montemorelos, Nuevo Leon, Mexico
Oshawa, Ontario, Canada

Edited by Marvin Moore
Designed by Tim Larson
Cover illustration by Eric Joyner
Type set in Century Schoolbook 10½/12½

Copyright © 1986 by
Pacific Press Publishing Association
Printed in United States of America
All Rights Reserved

Library of Congress Cataloging in Publication Data

Kangas, Janet Leigh.
Daughter of Son-light.

1. Diaz, Maria, 1915- . 2. Converts, Seventh-Day Adventists—United States—Biography. 3. Mediums—United States—Biography. I. McFadden, Elisabeth Spalding. II. Title.
BX6189.D53K36 1986 286.7'32'0924 [B] 86-17057
ISBN 0-8163-0670-2

86 87 88 89 90 • 5 4 3 2 1

Dedication

This book is lovingly dedicated to Fernanda Diaz (Maria) and her family:

Her daughter, Marie (Dulcita), and Marie's husband, Gary Steinbacher, with their two sons, Michael and Leroy;

Her sister, Juanita (Teresa), who brought Fernanda into the church before she died of cancer, and Juanita's four children, mothered by Fernanda after her death;

Her ex-husband Henrique, (now converted), and his wife, Carmen, their daughter Helen and her husband, John Sherman, and their two little daughters, Trisha and Jennie;

Fernanda's father and baby brother, Luis, and her mother, who preceded the two in death;

And to all the hundreds of Maria's converts, their children, and the thousands of "grandchildren" converts,

Who, never to be separated again by death, divorce, or distance, will all live together in God's heaven.

May the love in Maria's heart for her heavenly family embrace us all.

Acknowledgments

Recognition must be expressed to the author of Maria's first biography, Winnie Zerne. Without her book, *Maria, Daughter of Shadow,* there could be no sequel, for we could not have made the trip to Puerto Rico as she did, tracing and verifying Maria's strange adventures, and thus could not have begun this project. Winnie is now geographically unavailable and is therefore as unable to write this second book as we would have been to write the first.

We hope you will be pleased, Winnie.

Foreword

To know Maria Diaz is to love her at once, as her love for your soul penetrates you. To know Maria is also to become instantly integrated into her prayer life, for she is alert to every possibility of sharing her love story with Jesus.

When I was casually introduced as a writer to Maria, her immediate response was that she needed an author for a sequel to the first book of her biography, *Maria, Daughter of Shadow* (Pacific Press, 1975). "So trusting and open with me, a stranger," I thought.

I explained to Maria that I was too buried in my graduate work for this undertaking, and I mentioned other authors living in the area who might help her, even suggesting that she enlist the original author. Maria sadly shook her head. She had already pursued these possibilities.

Months later, however, I reached a difficult decision not to continue my studies during the summer of 1981, and I realized that I would still have about six weeks free. Maria's disappointed face immediately surfaced in my mind. I flirted with the idea of writing a book in only six weeks until classes called again. Could it be done?

I prayed, "Lord, I would rather you bring us together if it is Your desire to have me write this story. Please signal me by having our lives touch in some undeniable way, so that I will recognize Your leading."

At noon the next day I entered the snack shop on the campus of Andrews University and looked across the room. There was Maria, sitting at a table. Her eyes pulled me over, and as I sat down, we kept looking at each other in amazement.

"I asked God yesterday to have us meet again if He wants me to write your story," I said softly. "Have you found anyone?"

"Do you know that I told God just yesterday that I was through looking?" Maria responded. "I said, 'God, You know my story. If You want others to benefit from it, You will have to send me a writer; I give it all to You.' That was just yesterday too!" she repeated.

We sat quietly looking at each other for a moment, in reverence to God who designs a master plan and feeling grateful to each other for our mutual submission to Him which makes moments of direction and cooperative effort possible.

Now, after getting into Maria's story, I realize that this experience, a landmark in my life, was to Maria just another one of God's Go signs in her walk with Him.

Maria seems to have a succession of peak experiences that stem from three spiritual character traits she has developed: (1) constant alertness for possibilities (God would give us more if we would only ask), (2) expectant listening, and (3) eagerness to give God the glory for the answers.

Maria's story is written as she told it, a love for souls that pours from her great heart. I have tried not to dilute the straightforward, simple approach of her trust and faith. Never have I felt so helpless as a writer than when trying to translate into printed English the warm, emotional inflections of her Spanish accent, especially in the dialogue with Vicente and the birthday party. How I wish that every reader could feel the tenderness, excitement, and surprise that was evident on the tape I heard at least six times.

It would have been easy to sensationalize Maria's story. I have not, for to do so would have misrepresented her. Maria told me her experiences enthusiastically, yet calmly and reservedly, and I felt God gave the two of us this appointment together because of our compatibility in this approach.

Once, after she had engrossed me in her story so much that I ceased writing and could only listen, I asked her, "Maria, did you know that there are other authors who might not even have believed your stories?"

"Yes," she said. "That's one of the reasons God brought us together, isn't it?"

And so, reader, we bring you Maria's story.

—JLK

Contents

Maria
1981

Angels Unawares

Maria gave the door an extra tug. It slammed shut behind her, cutting out the swirling December snow.

"Why did you do that?" her sister Teresa chastened. "You were rude to that visitor."

"What visitor? I didn't see anybody." Maria frowned.

"You *must* have seen him, Maria. He walked up the steps with you, holding your arm. I looked out the window and saw him, and I wondered who you were bringing home for supper." Teresa flung opened the door and took a quick look up and down the New York street. There was no one in sight. The wind blew icy snow into her face. She strained to pull the door shut again and continued to scold her sister. "That's not like you to be so inhospitable, Maria."

"Honestly, Teresa, I didn't have anyone with me!"

"He had such soft brown eyes," Teresa insisted. "Such a kind face. He looked almost like an angel."

"An angel?" Maria gasped. Could that have been her own guardian angel guiding her across the busy street against the after-work traffic? Could he have placed an invisible arm under hers to see that she didn't slip as she ascended those icy stone steps? Maria remembered her feeling of complete safety as she wended her way home from work, hoping that her sister would have a hot drink ready to warm her frozen limbs. New York in winter offered little warmth to a Christian-book saleslady out ringing doorbells. The granite steps at home had not seemed slippery, either, she recalled. Could one of God's angels really have come to protect her?

It wasn't unusual for Maria to think of angels being present and sometimes visible. Ever since her mother's death when she was thirteen, Maria had been involved with the spirit world; only back then it had been the devil's angels. Born and raised in Puerto Rico, for over fifteen years Maria had been a spiritualist medium. And now that she had accepted Jesus as her Saviour, why shouldn't she take for granted that God's angels would protect her?

In all those years as a medium Maria had never placed a curse on any of her clients. Many of her fellow mediums used their powers to help themselves or to decree evil on others, but Maria had always tried to help people. She called forth her spirit "guides" to heal diseases, mend broken marriages, or help guide people to so-called happiness.

"Maria's spirits are good spirits," her clients used to say. "They will make you happy and healthy." Yet Maria had not been happy herself—not until she had turned her life over to Jesus Christ.

Oh, how she had fought doing that! Now, as she warmed her hands on the cup of hot cocoa that Teresa handed her, she recalled two occasions when her "good spirits" had turned on her, trying to snuff out her life. After resisting Teresa's urgent invitations to learn about Christ and what He had done for her, Maria's life had suddenly taken a plunge into tragedy. She and Henrique, her husband of nearly ten years, were divorced. Their daughter, Dulcita, was four years old.

Her turning in despair to her sister's teachings and beginning to study the Bible for herself had apparently angered Maria's spirit "guides." Not only did they refuse to respond when she tried to help someone in trouble, they began to threaten her own life. At night, when she tried to sleep, they awakened her with accusations, and finally one dark night she realized that a presence was in her room. Hands circled her throat to choke her. By the faint light filtering through the window she saw a picture of Jesus on the wall, and she prayed desperately, "Jesus, if You are real, as my sister says, please save me! Please save me!" Immediately the strangling sensation left. Then a peace such as Maria had never known seemed to fill the room. "Thank You, Jesus," she breathed, as she fell into a quiet sleep.

From that time on Maria dreamed only happy dreams. In one she seemed to see Jesus standing by her bed. She gazed in awe at His white-robed figure, of which she could see but the lower half. "Will you please tell me who You are?" she asked. Three times she repeated, "Are You Jesus?" Then she pleaded, "Jesus, if You are really my sister's God—the God of the Bible—won't You please give me a sign?" Then in her dream her eyes raised until they met His—beautiful eyes radiating love and tenderness. He slowly turned His hands and stretched them out toward her. The nail prints! She saw the nail prints in the palms of His hands! Maria gasped. That's what she had read in Teresa's Bible. It was really true. This was the Jesus who had died for her!

"It is Teresa's Jesus!" she cried out, waking herself up. "The Bible is true! He's real!" Falling to her knees beside the bed, she prayed, "Oh, dear Jesus. You saved me from those evil spirits. You died for me. I love you! I want to serve You."

Now, as she held the warm cup of cocoa in her hand, she spoke to Teresa across the table. "Remember, Sister, how Jesus took those bad spirits out of my life? Now I believe He has sent my special angel to guard me at my work."

"How well I remember!" Teresa answered. "Maria dear, you should not even think about those evil spirits. It was they who caused Señor Molino to put that curse on your marriage back in Puerto Rico. I should think you'd want to forget it all."

"I know, I know." Maria's voice sounded close to tears, and Teresa hastened to change the subject.

"Anyhow, I really do think you had an angel with you tonight, Maria." Teresa looked dreamy for a minute. "He wore a neat white suit, and he didn't look cold even in this snowy weather. His eyes were so beautiful—so kind."

"Then I hope that means Christ approves of my selling Christian books." Maria smiled.

"Oh, I'm sure He does," her sister agreed, as she cleared the table of their cups, wiped it clean, and began to set it for the evening meal. "The children will soon be in for supper," she reminded Maria, "and they'll be as hungry as wolves."

Maria Remembers

In spite of her resolution not to think of the past, Maria found herself remembering the early days of her marriage and the happiness she had known those three short months before Henrique left Puerto Rico for New York. "I'll send for you," he had promised, "as soon as I get my business established and find a place for us to live."

But the weeks stretched into months and the months into years. Even though Henrique wrote often at first, his letters offered no hint of when he might send for Maria to join him. Gradually his letters had become shorter and farther between.

Maria had kept their little home spotless. She busied herself with the clients who came to her for help and healing, calling on her spirit "guides" to aid her. She also started a lace and embroidery business that kept her hands busy, though not her mind. As she sat plying her needles she could not keep from thinking about the curse Señor Pascual Molino had put on her marriage.

"If you marry Henrique," he had sent word to her, "I will place a curse on your marriage. The union will last only three months." Maria shuddered as she remembered how this forty-year-old man, the head medium at her first temple, had tried to convince her that in a former life she had been his wife. Now the spirits were saying that she must marry him. Of course, she refused. She was only seventeen and could not see herself married to this older man. She changed temples at once, and it was at this second temple that she met Henrique Sanchez, a handsome young fellow medium. Two years later she married him.

Incensed, Señor Molino carried out his threat. The marriage, commenced under a curse, endured barely three months. In vain Maria pleaded with her own spirit "guides" to remove the curse, to send Henrique back to her. They did not respond. In desperation she consulted another spirit medium, an older man by the name of Señor Rafael. "Can you do anything to bring my husband back to me?" she begged with tears.

"Oh yes, I can," Señor Rafael assured her. "Your husband has been gone for many months—nearly two years, I see. But I can bring him back. It will cost you five dollars."

Maria paid the money, and he handed her a small bottle containing a colored liquid. "Shake this bottle every night and call your husband's name," he instructed. "Eventually, he will come."

Although Maria shook the bottle and called her husband's name faithfully, he did not come. She decided to sell their house and move in with her father, who lived alone. She saved the money Henrique sent from New York, as well as what she received from the sale of their house. "If he sends for me," she told her father, "I will have enough money to pay my way to New York."

As the second Christmas approached and Henrique neither came nor sent for her, she become depressed. People had even stopped asking, "When is Henrique coming back?" After her father left for work one morning she took out the bottle and shook it harder than ever, crying and calling Henrique's name. "Come home, Henrique. Oh, my darling, come home to me," she said over and over.

Downstairs, at work on her embroidery, she brushed away her tears. Then, just as she lifted her needle to begin to work, she heard the postman slip something through the mail slot in the front door. A white envelope lay on the floor beside her chair. Instantly, she recognized Henrique's handwriting. Jumping up, she clasped a letter to her breast. "Let it contain good news," she breathed as she tore it open.

"I'm coming home for Christmas," she read. He told when he would leave New York, what ship he would be on, and when it would arrive in Puerto Rico.

"Glory be!" Maria cried, laying aside her work. "I must go out and rent an apartment for Henrique and me to live in."

The day he arrived he looked even more handsome than when she had kissed him goodbye two years earlier, Maria thought. But in just a short time her happiness began to melt. She realized that something was different about her husband. She tried telling herself that it was because he had been away so long, that everything would be all right as soon as the feasting and merrymaking were over and they were alone in their apartment. She could hardly wait for that moment.

Henrique took her hand as they walked through the dark to the apartment she had so lovingly prepared for his return, but he did not speak. She switched on the light in the living room and turned to look into his eyes. "Is something wrong, Henrique?" she asked.

He stood there looking around the room. "No, no," he said, but he avoided her eyes. He walked through the entire apartment and then returned and took her in his arms. "You asked if something was wrong, Maria," he began. "After all you've done to make this apartment so pretty and comfortable, I'm ashamed to tell you that there is something wrong."

"What is it?" she cried, pushing him away so she could look into his troubled eyes.

He stared at the floor. "There's another girl in New York," he admitted. "I love her, too, and I came to ask you for a divorce."

His words fell like knives, piercing her heart. She

turned away in anguish. "How can you do this to me?" she cried. Anger replaced the hot tears in her eyes. He tried to take her in his arms again, but she pulled away, pounding on his shoulders. She ran into the bedroom and flung herself on the bed. He stood above her, trying to talk, but she covered her ears. She did not want to hear how he had met that girl, how he had fallen in love with her.

But what was he saying? In spite of herself, she grasped at the straw that he offered. "Now I am confused, Maria. You are so lovely. I seem to be in love with both of you. Can you give me time to work this out? Then maybe I will come back to you, Maria. Maybe I will."

Maria's face burns now as she thinks of how willingly she agreed to his plan. He returned to New York almost at once, and this time he had been true to his parting promise. "I will send for you, my darling." Within a few months he mailed her a ticket to New York.

Maria did everything she could to save the marriage. She even presented him with a baby daughter whom he loved very much. But it was all too late. Their marriage, cursed by a jealous suitor back in Puerto Rico, had failed. Henrique could not be happy with Maria. When his daughter, Dulcita, was four years old, he moved out of Maria's home.

Devastated, Maria turned to her sister's God, gave up her evil spirits, and found peace at last. But what did God want her to do with her life now? Time hung heavy on her hands. What could she do to take her mind from her troubles?

"If only I could find work where I could help people," she told Teresa. "The happiest times in my early life were when I could heal people, but I don't want to return to that life with those evil spirits. What *can* I do?"

Teresa had no suggestions, and Maria was becoming increasingly depressed, so she went to her minister. "Pastor, I want to know what God has in mind for me. I can't just sit at home brooding over my failed marriage. I'd like to help people who need me. Have you any ideas?" The pastor assured her that under the circumstances her feelings were normal, and he recommended patience, prayer, and more study of the Word of God. "I know God will guide you into the right work, Maria," he assured her. "In the meantime, let's both pray about it."

Several days later she returned to his home, still troubled with restlessness. "I think I have the answer for you, Maria," he said. "Do you know what you need to do?"

Maria leaned forward in her chair. "What is it, Pastor?"

"Colporteur work!"

"What's that?" Maria had never heard of colporteur work.

"A colporteur is someone who sells religious books from door to door. I did a few months of that kind of work before I entered the ministry. Often the people you sell to become very close to you. They tell you their troubles, and you can pray for them and guide them to Jesus."

"That sounds great!" Maria was enthusiastic. "When can I begin?"

"I like your spirit," the minister told her. He wrote the name and telephone number of the conference publishing director on a piece of paper and handed it to her. "Get an appointment to see him, and he will help you get started."

Maria's New Mission

A day or two later Maria went to the conference office and asked for the publishing director. However, he appeared skeptical when he heard her story. "You've only been a Christian for a short time," he said. "For now, study your Bible and pray about what God wants you to do. You should get to know Christ better before you attempt to sell books."

Maria went home discouraged, but her indomitable spirit soon surfaced. "If I could lead people to believe in the devil," she told herself, "I can certainly lead them to believe in Christ. I will sell books!" But instead of returning to the publishing director, she went to the Adventist Book Center.

"Which books are the best to sell?" she asked the clerk. He recommended the Spanish translation of *The Desire of Ages, The Great Controversy,* and *Counsels on Health,* and she bought a dozen of each.

Her little girl, Dulcita, was just six years old when Maria returned home lugging three boxes of books. "Oh, Mommy," she cried, "these are such beautiful books! May I read them?"

Maria smiled to herself. A six-year-old read those books? The child could barely read her first-grade primer. But since all they had was a phonograph with two religious records and a few books, Maria agreed. "All right, honey. You look at the pictures, and I will help you read them."

To Maria's amazement the little girl seemed to understand those adult books just as they were written. She grasped the story of Jesus' birth and life, and begged for more each night. "Rather grown-up bedtime stories," Maria thought, "but the best I could possibly give her."

On her first day out, Maria armed herself with two books of each kind and approached the first house, a small one set back from the road. A young mother with four small children clinging to her skirts answered the door. "What can I do for you?" she asked in Spanish.

"My name is Maria Diaz, and I am going house to house selling these beautiful books," Maria said, handing her a copy of *The Desire of Ages*.

The woman invited Maria into the house, and without even offering a chair, began turning the pages of the book. "I'm glad it's written in Spanish," she said. "That's my family's language, as you probably know."

"Yes," Maria said, "it's mine too. I'm from Puerto Rico."

The lady smiled. "Then you must meet my mother. She's also from Puerto Rico, although we've lived in New York for many years." She turned the pages of the book more slowly, reading a line or two here and there.

"This is a beautiful book," she said, handing it back. "Let me see the others." Maria handed her *The Great Controversy*. After scanning it briefly she said, "This must be a history book. Can you tell me what it's about?"

"No, I'm sorry, I can't," Maria admitted. "I just bought them last week. Someone told me these books are really good. That's why I'm selling them. I'm going to read them as soon as I find time." Maria brought out the medical book and handed it to the woman.

"This, too, is beautiful!" the young woman cried. "How much are all three?" Without waiting for Maria to answer, she turned toward the back of the house. "Mother," she called, "leave those dishes until later. Come see these books written in Spanish. They're so attractive." Her mother hurried into the room, drying her hands on her apron. She pushed strands of hair out of her face as she looked at the books. "I like these books," she told her daughter a few minutes later. "I think we should call in all of our relatives to see them."

"My name is Sophia," the young woman told Maria, "and this is my mother, Elena." She motioned to a chair. "Please sit down while I call everyone to come see your books."

Maria sold all three dozen books at that first house! But she wasn't through with her customer yet. More than sales, she longed to win souls. "Since I haven't read these books either," she suggested to the young mother, "maybe we could read them together."

"I'd like that," Sophia said. "When can you come?" Maria arranged to spend an hour each weekday morning, reading the books with her new friend.

One day Sophia said, "Maria, you must have other books like these. Bring me more."

"I'll go to the store and see what I can find," Maria said.

With the money from the sale of the first three dozen books Maria returned to the Adventist Book Center and bought six dozen new books. Soon she had made enough profit to add other books, increasing her sales line, and she went door-to-door, saturating her neighborhood for several blocks around her home with books about Jesus and salvation.

"It's a success, a big success!" Maria exclaimed to her sister. "My business is good. God is using me to help others learn to know Jesus. I'm so happy, Teresa. Back when I served as a spirit medium I could only help people in *this* life. Now I'm helping them for eternity!"

Nearly a year had passed when the conference publishing director conducted a colporteur rally at Maria's church, and Maria attended. "Hello, Maria," he said smiling, and he shook hands with her. "Do you think you are ready to start selling books now? I could go out with you next week to get you started."

"Oh, sir, I have been selling those books for several months," Maria told him.

"What!" he exclaimed. "Who took you out?"

"I just took myself out, and God blessed me," Maria said.

The man's mouth dropped open. "How did you sell those books?"

"For cash, of course," Maria replied.

"I mean, what did you say to the people?"

Maria told him how she had canvassed the streets around her house. "I referred many people to the Spanish minister," she said, "and so far eight people have been baptized from my neighborhood of Pentecostals and Catholics."

The publishing director's face grew serious. "I am more convinced than ever that this is God's business, not man's," he said soberly. Later, when he took Maria to colporteur rallies and had her tell her story, he would add with tears in his eyes, "It is God's work, fellow colporteurs, not ours."

Yet not all of Maria's experiences turned out so smoothly. One day while canvassing a man and his wife in their living room about *The Great Controversy,* Maria noticed that the husband had not spoken and that a frown creased his brow. Suddenly he snatched her briefcase, grabbed her by the arm, and shoved her out the door. "If you don't get out of here, you'll go out like the books!" he yelled. "God, when He gets mad, He kills!" Then he opened her briefcase and threw every item, piece by piece, onto the muddy ground.

"No! No!" his wife screamed as the man slammed the door shut.

As Maria crouched down picking up her books, she noticed two black shoes planted beside her. Looking up, she saw a man with a briefcase standing in front of her.

"You fell?" he asked, offering his hand. He helped her to her feet and then stooped and began picking up her books, wiping each one off as he put it back into her briefcase. "Are you a missionary?" he asked.

"Yes," Maria answered.

"What kind?"

"A Seventh-day Adventist."

"Oh!" his face lit up. "Do you sell Ellen G. White's books?"

"Yes."

"I'm a Pentecostal minister," he explained. "Come home with me and meet my wife. I'd like to look over your books."

Maria followed the man to his home.

"Come here, honey," he called to his wife as they entered the house. "I've found a young woman with those books I've been looking for so long." After he had introduced Maria to his wife he said, "I've never read any books as inspiring as those Ellen White wrote. I want to preach from them. There's so much she can teach our people." He hesitated, then added, "Well, about everything except the Sabbath, that is. On that the author is wrong."

Maria smiled. "What he doesn't know," she thought, "is that everyone in his neighborhood already has these books!"

Maria soon learned that a friend had loaned *The Desire of Ages* to this minister years before. He had read it, returned it, and had since lost track of the friend. For months he had been looking for more of Ellen White's books. He promptly bought four of Maria's books and ordered four more.

"I guess God wanted to teach me that after every fall He will pick me up and lead me to something better!" Maria said that evening after she told Teresa what happened.

Souls, Not Sales

Maria often suffered arthritis in the damp New York climate. Sometimes she longed for her native Puerto Rico, but she felt that America was a better place to raise her little girl. Besides, Teresa and her family lived in Maria's home with her, so she stayed. One morning, after her malady had crippled her and forced her to stay in bed for several months, she began longing to win a soul for the Lord. Teresa was at work, the children in school.

"Please, dear Jesus," Maria prayed, "give me at least one soul today. Show me how to win one soul for You, even though I must stay in bed like this."

Presently she heard a knock on her door. "Come in," Maria called, and a young Puerto Rican woman named Merita stepped inside.

"I've come to pay you for my books," Merita said, and then she glanced around the room. "Maria, this will never do," she exclaimed. "You must get well. You are doing too much good with your books to stay sick like this."

"I'm trying to learn patience," Maria answered. "I know God will heal me in His own good time."

"How are things with you, anyway?" Merita asked. "Do lots of people owe you money like I did?"

Maria acknowledged that quite a few customers still owed for their books. "But I am more interested in their souls than their money, Merita," she said. "If only I could get out of here and win souls. At least you are already a Christian." She sighed, forcing a smile.

"Yes," Merita answered, "thanks to you, I am a Christian." Then her eyes fell on a pile of *Signs of the Times* lying nearby. She picked one up. "These are fast becoming out of date, Maria," she said. "Would you mind if I sold them for you?"

"Imagine," Maria thought to herself, "this girl hardly knows me and she certainly knows nothing about that magazine. How can she sell it?" Then she remembered her own experience. She sold books when *she* knew almost nothing about them. Aloud, she said, "Why not?"

Merita took fifty magazines, and in a few days she had sold every one. She brought Maria the money. Maria thanked her and offered to share the money. "Oh, no," Merita cried, "I did it to help you. In fact, I have another idea. Why don't you give me a list of the people who owe you money, and I will call them on the phone and tell them that since you are sick they should bring their money to you." Thinking it over, Maria decided she might have an opportunity to talk with each client about Jesus if Merita followed her plan, so she agreed.

For a few weeks this kept Maria satisfied, but once again the old longing to be involved in bringing "just one soul" to Christ swept over her. She prayed, "Lord, You know my body aches all over, but my heart burns for souls. Give me one soul, here from my bed. Tell me what to do, Lord, and I will do it."

As Maria finished praying she heard her neighbors next door talking in unusually high-pitched voices. "They must have visitors," she thought, "and it sounds like an argument is going on." Inspiration struck her. "I can walk that far," she told herself. "I can go to those neighbors." She'd never thought of going to them with the books. They just didn't seem interested in religious things. Although the wife knew Maria sold books, she had never asked about them.

Painfully, Maria slid out of bed, put on her housecoat

and slippers, and brushed her hair. She picked up a copy of *The Desire of Ages* in one hand, and by hanging onto the walls with the other and wobbling along, she managed to reach the neighbors' house and ring the bell. When the wife opened the door she cried, "Why, Mrs. Diaz, I thought you were bedridden. Come sit down; you'll hurt yourself!"

Sinking into the nearest chair, Maria told her, "I felt so lonely. I forced myself to come here. I brought this book along for you and your guests to see."

Whatever the argument had been between them, it was now forgotten. The husband took the book and examined it. "Why haven't you shown us this book before?" he demanded. "I would have bought one long ago." The guests expressed an interest, too, and Maria sold two copies of *The Desire of Ages* for cash that morning. Later she started Bible studies with her neighbors. However, after a few months Maria moved to Massachusetts for Dulcita's schooling. She asked another church member to continue studying with neighbors after she moved away.

Fortunately, in Massachusetts Maria's health improved. After she and Dulcita had lived there for a little over a year she suggested that they return to New York for a visit. "I think I can spare a week from selling books to visit your Aunt Teresa," she said, "and you could see your father."

Dulcita was ecstatic. "When can we go, Mother?" she asked, dancing up and down.

"I think we could leave in the morning," Maria said.

"Wow!" Dulcita exclaimed. Even though her father had visited her in Massachusetts, she still wanted to see more of him. "Isn't it nice that school is out," she said. "Now I can spend several days with Daddy." Dulcita flashed her mother a quick smile and ran to her room to pack her suitcase.

Dulcita spent the weekend with her father. Teresa had moved to a new neighborhood, so Maria was unable to visit many of her former clients, but she thoroughly enjoyed the few days with her sister.

On Sabbath afternoon Maria took a trolley over to her old neighborhood and attended an afternoon service at the church she formerly attended. She walked in a little late and immediately realized that a baptism was already in progress. A man and woman stood in front with baptismal robes on. The man's testimony reached Maria's ears as she slid into a rear pew.

"How I wish that Mrs. Diaz could be here," he said. "God and Mrs. Diaz brought us here." He glanced at his wife, who nodded in agreement. Suddenly Maria recognized them as her old neighbors, the couple she had begun Bible studies with when she was bedridden with arthritis. Tears of joy began to roll down her cheeks. When the man finished his testimony, Maria stood up so he could see her. "I *am* here," she said. "God brought me here to witness this baptism." The man and his wife gasped, then rushed down the aisle and threw their arms around Maria. Tears ran down their cheeks.

"Thank You, Lord, for answering my lonely prayer that day so long ago," Maria whispered as the minister lowered them into the water. "You gave me, not one soul, but two!"

Another Angel Appears

Maria had not wanted to leave New York. She had many friends, both in her neighborhood and in the church, and she hated to transfer her Bible studies to someone else. But Henrique presented a problem that she felt she could not solve if they continued living in the same city.

"You're a big girl now, honey," Henrique told Dulcita when she reached her twelfth birthday. "You can make your own decisions, and you don't have to live with your mother all of the time. Why don't you come live with me? You could just go visit her sometimes like you've been doing with me all these years."

Maria decided she must protect her child from being drawn into the spirit world from which she herself had escaped with difficulty. So at the minister's suggestion she and Dulcita visited South Lancaster, Massachusetts, where the church had good schools for Dulcita to attend all the way through college.

Maria returned to New York alone. "Both of us loved it up there," she told Teresa. "The people were so friendly. Elder Vernon Siver found us a room with a Mrs. Mary MaKenny, and she offered to keep Dulcita for a few days so she could begin school right away. I came back for our things."

"Do you have an apartment or a house up there?" Teresa asked.

"Not yet. Mrs. MaKenny wants us to stay with her until we find a place."

Teresa looked sad. "I'm sure you'll be happy there, Maria," she said. "And I know it's best for Dulcita, but we'll surely miss you here."

Maria gave her sister a hug and began packing her things. Teresa helped in silence. Maria knew she hated to lose the close companionship the two had shared since Maria had become a Christian. Suddenly, it swept over her too. She would be leaving all her friends and relatives, moving into one room with her twelve-year-old daughter, saying goodbye to everything that was familiar, all to save her daughter from her father's religion! For a few moments she felt as if she could not make the break, but thoughts of Dulcita getting drawn into spiritualism spurred her on.

As Maria left for the train station she thought of Abraham in Bible times. Like him, she had cut the ties. She was going out, not knowing whither she went, but she must trust God to take care of her and her precious daughter.

The train was almost ready to pull out when she reached the station, but with her suitcase and two lamps in her hands she could not open the door onto the train. "Oh, dear, what shall I do?" she asked herself.

"Wait! Wait! I'm coming. I'll help you!" Maria turned to see a tall, well-built young man with light brown hair running toward her. He was dressed in a white summer suit, and his kind brown eyes were set in the most handsome face she had ever seen. "Give me the lamps." He lifted the lamps from her hand. At the same time he pushed open the door and held it with his foot. After she entered the train he handed one of the lamps back to her and took her suitcase, leading her down the aisle to an empty seat. There seemed to be a refinement in his manner. She felt she had encountered him someplace before, but she couldn't remember where. His ready smile gave her a feeling of confidence, as if to say, "I'll take care of you now. Just relax and leave things to me." Yet he had hardly spoken a word since showing her the seat she should take. The young man took the seat next to her, yet neither of them said much.

As the train sped along, Maria noticed some of the other passengers taking out their lunches. "Oh, dear," she thought, "I forgot to make one for myself." She did not mention this to the young man, yet he seemed to sense it. When a porter came by selling sandwiches, he bought two, along with two bottles of orange juice. He handed her one of the sandwiches and a bottle of juice.

"Oh, no thank you," Maria said politely. He insisted, so she reached for her purse.

"Never mind. Just eat it." His voice sounded kind, yet authoritative. He began to eat his sandwich, glancing her way to be sure she was eating hers. Maria thanked him and bit into the sandwich.

Finally, to make conversation, she asked, "Where are you going, young man?"

"To Worcester, Massachusetts," he replied.

"I'm going there, too!" she exclaimed. The man said nothing, and he didn't seem to be much for talk, so Maria settled down for a nap. Shortly after she fell asleep, she awoke to see the man stand up and take down the lamps from the shelf. "Are we in Worcester already?" she asked. "I didn't think I had slept that long."

"No," the young man told her. "This train goes to Boston. We have to change here for Worcester."

"Really?" Maria looked around her. Other passengers were getting off too. "I'm so glad you told me," she said as she picked up her suitcase. "I'd have gone on to Boston, and I don't have money enough for a ticket back."

The man glanced back over his shoulder as Maria followed him down the aisle. "Your daughter is waiting," he said, and he gave her the most beautiful smile she thought she had ever seen.

"How did he know that?" Maria wondered. She hadn't mentioned her daughter, but she hesitated to question him about himself or how he knew things. He just seemed to be so special—"so out of this world"—Maria told herself as she followed him off the train.

Her guide took her immediately to the next train. He seemed to know exactly what to do, and Maria followed him in blind trust. He chose a seat about the center of the car as he had done on the first train, placed her lamps on the rack and her suitcase at her feet. "Why, he doesn't even have a suitcase himself," Maria gasped. She glanced out the window at the gathering darkness. She felt so safe and secure on this train. It never entered her mind to question the conductor or check the signs to make sure that she was on the right train. Her self-appointed guardian seemed to be taking care of everything for her.

She turned to thank him for his help. He wasn't there! She glanced quickly up and down the aisle. He wasn't in sight. The train was pulling out, and he wasn't there!

"It couldn't have been more than thirty seconds that I was looking out that window," she told Dulcita and Mrs. MaKenny when she reached South Lancaster. "Somehow, I sensed he was special, and I wanted to keep my eyes on him. But he just faded from sight, in the twinkling of an eye—the snap of my finger."

Dulcita spoke first. "It must have been your guardian angel, Mommy," she declared matter-of-factly. "You know God always sends him when you need him."

Maria hugged her daughter and smiled over her head at Mrs. MaKenny. "Yes, I'm sure it was." Maria could not hold back the tears of joy. She knew that guarding her daughter's spiritual life by bringing her here from New York had been the right decision. And to think that the great God of heaven thought so much of her that He sent a special angel to guide her and help her get on the right train!

A Young Girl's Faith

Dulcita's first realization of the spirit world came when she was about eight years old. One day, while they still lived in New York, she wandered into the kitchen to find her mother burning books in the deep sink.

"Mommy, what are you doing?" she asked, wide-eyed.

"I'm getting rid of these books," Maria told her daughter. "They belong to the devil, and I won't have them in my house any longer." Only a few months earlier Maria had accepted Christ into her life, and now she wanted to break all connection with her former life of serving the devil and his demons.

"The devil's books, Mommy? Then why did you have them?"

Dulcita's curiosity wasn't to be satisfied with a short explanation, so Maria sat down and told her about her early life in Puerto Rico and how she had been a spirit medium. "I was very stubborn, Dulcita," she admitted. "Even after Aunt Teresa became a Christian and tried to lead me to Jesus, I refused to listen, but now that you and I have come to love Jesus I just want to leave all that wicked life behind me." She purposely avoided telling Dulcita of the times the demons had tried to kill her. She didn't want to frighten the child. Yet Dulcita instinctively drew closer to her mother.

"Mommy," she cried, "will those bad spirits come back

to bother me when it's dark?"

"Oh no, darling. You mustn't worry about that. Jesus will take care of you so they can't hurt you." Had she told the child too much? she wondered. Would she be afraid?

Maria's fears came true. Dulcita began to cry every night when Maria put her to bed. "I'm afraid of those evil spirits," she told Maria. She seemed terrified of the dark, so Maria began leaving a small light burning in her room. Still, Dulcita sometimes cried out in her sleep, "They're after me, Mommy! Come save me, Mommy!" Maria would take her Bible and open it to the ninety-first psalm. She would read it to her daughter, and then if Dulcita still seemed afraid she would lay the open Bible across her chest and sit holding her hand until she fell asleep.

In the daytime Dulcita forgot about the bad spirits. She kept very active thinking up pranks to play on her cousins who lived with them. Consequently, Dulcita received her share of spankings, but she soon learned to be sorry for her "sins" and to ask Jesus to forgive her. She grew up with a close relationship to her Friend, Jesus.

There was little money in the household now. But whenever Dulcita received a dime she always asked to have it changed into ten pennies so that she could put one in the church envelope for tithe. She carefully printed her name on the envelope, and when there were five or more pennies in it, she wrote the amount on the envelope and turned it in at church. Often, when things went wrong at home, she would remind Maria, "Pray, Mommy. Pray." Maria felt happy to see her daughter developing into such a dedicated Christian.

One day nine-year-old Dulcita ran upstairs to find her mother. By this time three families of Dulcita's cousins lived in the same house. "Mommy, all my cousins have toy watches," she cried. "May I have one too?"

"How much do they cost?" Maria asked.

"Only ten cents."

"Darling," Maria said, "I don't have even ten cents."

"You don't have ten cents, Mommy? Then let's pray." Dulcita began tugging her mother to her knees.

Stalling for time, Maria asked, "What do you want to say?"

"I'm going to ask Jesus for ten cents," she replied, and she knelt beside her mother. "Dear Jesus, I need ten cents to buy a toy watch. Won't you please send it to me? Thank You, Jesus."

Maria found herself praying too. "Lord, honor her faith." But she could see no way to provide even ten cents on this particular day.

Confident that her prayer would be answered, Dulcita ran downstairs to play with her six cousins. They were all in Uncle Santos's apartment. Uncle Santos sat in his easy chair watching the children compare watches. He saw Dulcita standing to one side, looking sad. "Don't you have a watch, Dulcita?" he asked.

"No."

"Why don't you have a watch, Dulcita?"

"Mommy doesn't have ten cents for me to buy one."

"Oh." Uncle Santos reached into his pocket. "Here's ten cents, honey. Go buy a watch!"

"Thank you! Thank you!" Dulcita dashed toward the door. But then she stopped. "Jesus told you to give me this dime," she remarked. Uncle Santos looked puzzled, but she just ran out the door and across the street to buy her toy watch.

Moments later, Dulcita came back and ran upstairs. "Mommy! Mommy! I have a watch. Uncle Santos gave me the money to buy it. I didn't even ask him for it. Jesus just told him to give it to me. Let's kneel down and thank Jesus, shall we?" Maria smiled and knelt with her little daughter. "What faith the child has!" she thought.

Maria felt grateful to her sister Teresa, who had taken Dulcita to church even before Maria's own conversion. She remembered thinking, before she gave her own heart to the Lord, "I don't want my daughter to go to that church and become a fanatic, always talking about Jesus." But she had let Dulcita go, believing that she needed to be with her cousins, and reasoning, "She's too young to learn that strange religion, anyhow." What a change in Maria's heart since she had found Jesus and realized the importance of early childhood impressions!

While they still lived in Manhattan, Dulcita had to ride a subway to church school. Teresa's children attended public school because her husband was not a Christian and said it was foolish to spend money for school when they could go free. So Maria always took her daughter to the train station and saw her safely on the car. During second grade Dulcita fell and cracked a bone in her knee. It became very difficult for her to board the steps of the train, yet she insisted she must not miss school. Maria agreed to accompany her all the way to school for three months until her knee healed, even though this made Maria quite late getting out to sell her books.

"It hurts so bad," Dulcita cried one day after they had boarded the train. "I'm getting sick all over, Mommy." Maria glanced at her pale face and decided to take her off the crowded train at the next stop.

They found a ladies' room at the station, and Dulcita lost her breakfast. "Let's go on, Mommy," she insisted. "I feel better now, and I don't want to miss school. If I ask Jesus to help me, I know that I can go on to school." Right there in the subway station Dulcita sent up a prayer of faith to her Friend and continued on her way to school. Maria marveled at her daughter's courage. In addition to the pain, Dulcita became nauseated if the train was too crowded. When Dulcita could stand it no longer, she and Maria would get off the train, find a ladies' room where Dulcita could recover, and then wait for another train. For three months Dulcita and Maria endured this trying situation so that Dulcita would not have to drop out of church school.

At the age of nine, Dulcita begged to be baptized. She

seemed to feel that she couldn't go to heaven without baptism, so Maria consented, even though she felt her daughter was very young. When Elder Charles Keymer lowered the slim little girl into the water, she came up with a smile that, to Maria, looked like an angel's smile.

When Henrique realized how serious his daughter felt about joining the Seventh-day Adventist Church, he tried to interest her in spiritualism. Dulcita told her Mother, "I love Daddy and I hate to hurt him, yet I always remember how scared I got when you first told me you had been a spiritualist medium. I'm afraid I'll have those nightmares again."

It was at this point that Maria decided she must move away from New York. It was bad enough being torn between two parents. Dulcita should not be torn between two religions. So they moved to Massachusetts.

After they found an apartment, Henrique paid them a visit. One night after Dulcita had gone to bed he sat on the sofa next to Maria. "I made a mistake, Maria," he said. "I cannot live without my daughter. I'm sorry for what I did to bring on our divorce. Won't you please forgive me and take me back?" He reached for her hand.

Maria's heart skipped a beat. She really did love Henrique, but her head told her to check into this more thoroughly. She asked him how he would handle the religious side of their lives. His answer convinced her that he still intended to cling to his spiritualist beliefs. Sadly, she released her hand from his. "Spiritualism and Adventism will never mix," she said. "It would not work for me to marry you again. Why don't you go back to New York and find a woman who believes the way you do and marry her?"

He lowered his eyes to the floor. For a long time he did not answer. Then he smiled at her. "I guess you're right, Maria. It would never work." The next morning he returned to New York.

Dulcita's Faith Grows

Dulcita continued to maintain a close relationship with her Friend, Jesus Christ, and as she entered her early teens she looked forward to attending the academy at South Lancaster, near her home.

Occasionally she made trips back to New York to visit her father, and he nearly always took her shopping, buying her clothes such as shoes and coats, and even a flute and piano. He smiled on her proudly as she modeled the blouses and skirts she chose for school and the dresses she liked for church. During one shopping trip he bought her a beautiful gray princess-style coat for winter. She needed a winter coat, and she proudly took it home to show Maria. Stroking the silver fox collar and letting her hand run down over the light gray fabric of the coat, she slipped it to model for her mother. "Don't you just love this coat, Mother?" she asked.

Her mother kept silent, appraising the coat.

"Mother?" she asked again.

Her mother studied the beautiful garment. "Yes, darling," she finally agreed, "it is beautiful. Expensive, too, no doubt."

Dulcita looked at her mother. "You really don't like it, do you?"

"Well, I think it's a little too old for you. Don't you see? It's more for a college girl or an adult woman."

"But I need it." Dulcita's face fell. "You know I need it. Can't I at least wear it for church?"

"Well, I won't say that you can't, Dulcita. But I don't like to see you wear something that will make you grow up so fast. I would prefer to find you a simpler wrap. The other girls might be envious, and some might think it's comical for you to wear something so out of place. Either way, you wouldn't be able to forget about yourself for a moment while you wear it, and that's not like our Jesus. The decision is yours. I just want you to pray about it and then see how you feel."

The next morning Dulcita admitted, "I guess I have to agree with you, Mother. It is too old for me. Perhaps we should just put it away until I'm older." As she brought the coat down to be packed in mothballs and a plastic cover, she stroked the fur again. "It feels so soft." She lifted it to her face and then handed it to her mother and helped smooth it into the plastic bag.

"I'll buy you a coat more suitable for your age before winter," Maria promised.

But winter blew in with a sudden gust one November afternoon, and Dulcita rushed home through the snow flurries, hugging her thin spring jacket around her. "Oh, dear," she wailed, "I can't go to church tomorrow in this light jacket if it's as cold as this. I nearly froze getting home."

"I'm sorry, Dulcita. I don't know what to do. I thought surely I'd have the money for your new coat by now."

Dulcita put her arm around her mother, "I know. It's not your fault," she sighed. "I should have had Daddy buy me a more suitable coat." Then she brightened and turned toward her mother. "We've forgotten to pray about this, you know. I'm sure that Jesus wants me to go to church. He'll provide a way if we ask Him."

Together they knelt down. Dulcita prayed first. "Jesus, it's so cold outside, and I do want to go to church tomorrow. You know that I can't wear this spring jacket, nor can I wear that fancy woman's coat. Please send me a warm coat, one right for a young girl my age, and send it tonight, if You can. Thank You, Lord Jesus!"

Maria drew in her breath as she realized Dulcita's faith remained as strong as the time she had prayed for a dime to buy a toy watch. She hardly knew how to word her own prayer, for she could not see any way to change the situation. So she just said, "Jesus, please consider her prayer, so sincere and trusting it is." In her heart she silently prayed, "And give me half the faith that my daughter has!"

As she rose from her knees it seemed that a voice spoke to her. Why not take that coat to the dormitory and sell it to one of the older college girls? It was Friday afternoon. There was the housework and cooking yet to do, but the voice insisted, *"Do it now."*

"Dulcita," Maria said, "do you think that you could manage the Friday work? I have an errand to take care of right away."

Without asking what Maria planned to do, Dulcita said, "Of course I can, Mother. What are you planning for Sabbath dinner?"

Maria outlined a menu, then mentioned a few tasks yet to be done around the house. Dulcita wrote them down. She saw her mother take the fancy coat from the closet, but she didn't ask questions. She knew that God would somehow work it all out, and she watched her mother brave the storm as she went out the door.

"Wonderful girl," Maria thought as she plodded through the storm toward the women's dormitory. "She didn't even ask me where I was going. I hated to tell her, in case my idea won't work." But she prayed as she hurried along the sidewalk that was rapidly turning white with snow. "Oh, Lord, send somebody who needs a nice winter coat—some college girl who has the money to pay for it right now."

As she entered the dormitory and brushed the snow

from her bundle, the dean of women came through her office door. She spotted the coat showing through the plastic on Maria's arm.

"What a beautiful coat, Mrs. Diaz! Whose is it?" she asked.

Maria told her the whole story, even to Dulcita's prayer of faith, and then added, "I thought perhaps there might be some young woman in your dormitory who might need a coat like this."

The dean removed the coat from its plastic cover, held it up, and examined it. "You're right," she said. "This coat is too old for a girl of fourteen. Here. Help me into it; I'd like to try it on."

Maria held the coat for her and noted as she slipped it on that it was a perfect fit for the dean herself. "Isn't it lovely!" the dean exclaimed. She turned from side to side, admiring the coat in a full-length mirror. Then she turned to Maria. "You won't need to go any further. I'll buy the coat from you."

Maria could hardly believe her ears. She took the money that the dean handed her and was turning to go out the door when the dean said, "Do you have a way downtown to buy another coat for Dulcita?"

"No, but it's not far. I can walk."

"I should say not!" the dean replied. "Not in this weather," and she went to get her car keys.

A couple of hours later Maria and the dean burst through Maria's apartment door. "Dulcita," her mother cried, "your prayers have been answered. Come see your new coat!"

Dulcita hurried into the living room carrying a dust cloth just as her mother drew a navy blue coat from a large paper bag. "Oh!" she exclaimed. "It's lovely!" She ran her hand over one of the sleeves. "I want to try it on."

The dean slipped the coat around Dulcita's shoulders, then turned her around and looked at her. "You look beautiful," she said.

Dulcita twirled around and around in her new coat, "I love it! It's such a pretty navy blue!" She paused and looked in a mirror and ran her hand along the edge of the collar. "It's got such pretty pink stitching on the collar, and it's a wide collar, just like the girls are wearing now."

All three of them laughed, and the the dean said, "It's a perfect fit, Dulcita." She glanced at her watch. "It's only an hour until sundown. I'd better be going. I'll see you in your new coat in church tomorrow."

After the dean left, Maria explained to Dulcita how she had sold the coat with its fur collar to the dean. "Isn't God good?" she said.

Dulcita tugged at her mother's arm. "I want to kneel down right now and thank Jesus for a perfect new coat."

Maria's Windows of Heaven

A few months after arriving in Massachusetts, Maria and Dulcita were able to move out of Mrs. MaKenny's house into a small apartment that Maria found near the campus of Atlantic Union College. The rent was modest, affordable on their meager budget, Maria thought. However, in spite of good sales and Henrique's faithful support for Dulcita, she sometimes found that there was "too much month left at the end of the money." Yet she always paid a faithful tithe, claiming God's promise in Malachi 3:10 to open the windows of heaven if she would be faithful. In offerings she gave as much as she could, but never as much as she would have liked. "Colporteurs are usually poor in money, but rich in blessings from on high," she told Dulcita, adding, "First we pay the tithe, then the tuition for your Christian education. If anything's left over we'll buy the shoes you need or my new glasses." Dulcita grew up living by these principles.

God did take care of them and blessed them. He also took care of His tithe and offerings. One Sabbath morning Maria decided to visit New York. Leaving Dulcita at home, she took a train to New York, then caught a subway to the church at Queens on Long Island. As she hurried down the subway stairs one of her shoestrings came untied and she laid her Bible, hymnal, and small red purse on the step beside her while she retied the shoe string. Because she was running late, she snatched up the Bible and hymnal, but failed to pick up the little purse.

It wasn't until offeringtime at church that she missed it. She remembered, with a sinking heart, that she had left it at the subway station. It contained her tithe in an envelope, some offering money, and even the rent money due on Monday. Over $200 in all!

Trying to calm herself, she reasoned, "It won't help for me to miss Sabbath School and church, because it won't be there now, anyhow." She decided to call on Jesus for help. "Lord, remember my tithe and the money I need to live on. You always bless me and are good to me, so I leave it in Your hands." She believed that God would take care of her money, and then she forgot about it and enjoyed the services. She decided that if God did not return the purse, He would provide money some other way.

After church Maria asked Sylvia, a girl she knew quite well, to loan her enough money to get home on the subway. Sylvia looked surprised, but reached into her purse to get the money. Maria thought she should explain, so she told her what had happened. "Oh, but you're not going alone," Sylvia cried. "I'll go with you to the subway station; then you are coming home with me to dinner."

The two women approached the cashier at the station. "Did anyone turn in a purse here?" Maria asked.

"What kind of purse?"

"A small red purse." Maria indicated the size with her hands.

"What was inside?" he asked.

"House keys, an envelope with money for my church, and about $200 besides. Most of that was my rent money."

The man smiled and reached under the counter. "Young woman, you must live right," he said, and he handed Maria her purse. "I'd never have dreamed anyone in New York City would've returned a lost purse containing over $200, but here it is!"

Sylvia gasped. "Is the money inside?"

"Of course," Maria said. "God never does things half way."

"But you haven't even looked inside," Sylvia said.

Not until Maria pulled out the tithe envelope and showed her the $200 in cash did she believe it. "It's a miracle!" she cried. "And in New York City it's a modern miracle!"

"I knew God would do it," Maria said. "I prayed in church and asked Him to, you know."

Selling Christian books in sparsely settled Massachusetts was a bigger challenge than it had been in New York. After struggling along for nearly a year, and with sales diminishing rather than increasing, Maria often spread her money out on the bed and called Dulcita to her side to pray with her about it. "Lord," she would say, "You are giving us money for our expenses only, but by faith we are going to take out Your tithe first, and what's left we'll use for ourselves. Whatever comes, will come. I leave it up to You to send more money if You think we need it."

Usually there seemed no way to make the money meet the bills, yet Maria's and Dulcita's faith grew as time after time they watched extra money come in the mail. Someone would pay up an old book bill, or Aunt Teresa would send money for a birthday gift. Once two twenty-dollar bills came in a plain white envelope with no name attached. "It can only be dropping from those windows in heaven, Mommy," Dulcita exclaimed.

After struggling for a year trying to sell books in Massachusetts, Maria decided to accept steady employment in a book bindery. "It will mean a regular paycheck," she told her daughter, "and I can be home with you more." But after a few months she and several other employees were laid off. "I'm losing money," the manager told them. "Times are hard. People are just not ordering books."

Maria's small savings soon disappeared, and she decided to spend a Sabbath day fasting and praying for a job. As the sun sank in the western sky at the end of the day her spirits also seemed to sink. "Why am I so discouraged?" she asked herself. "I should have faith. I should know that God is going to answer my prayers." She decided that the devil was behind her depression, so she prayed, "Lord, help me to resist Satan and give me faith to believe that a job will be waiting on Monday." Her depression lifted immediately, and her heart sang. "It's as though I actually have a job already," she told Dulcita.

All day Sunday Maria went about her housework singing and praising God for taking care of her needs. Monday morning she asked Mrs. MaKenny if she would take her to town. "I need to go to work, Mary," she told her friend. "I have a job, you know."

"You have a job, Maria? Who gave it to you?"

"The Lord Jesus."

"I mean, where will you work?"

"I don't know yet, but I am going to the unemployment office to find out."

Mrs. MaKenny scratched her head and looked at Maria. "All right," she said at last. "Let's go."

On the way to the unemployment office Maria asked Mary to pull the car to the side of the road for a moment.

"Lord," Maria prayed, "thank You for the job You have given me. Help me prove myself good. Please let me keep this job a long time. I need it to pay my tithe and offerings, and I need it for me and to keep my little girl in church school. Amen."

Mary stared at Maria. "If you have a job, why are we going to the unemployment office?" she asked.

"I thought I told you." Maria seemed surprised. "I know I have a job, but I'm not sure where. I have to check with the unemployment office." Mary drove on in silence. Maria knew what she was thinking: Most people in South Lancaster are out of work. A depression is sweeping the country. But still Maria feels sure that God has given her a job! They drove on to the unemployment office.

The little balding man behind the counter brushed the

sweat from his forehead. He adjusted his half-moon glasses and peered over them. "Oh, Mrs. Diaz, it's you again. I don't know what I am going to do with you because you didn't work long enough at your old job to collect unemployment or enough residency to go on welfare. You don't have a job, and I can't help you."

Maria smiled at him. "You can do something!"

The man turned his eyes on Maria and flashed a tiny smile. "I don't think it will work, but I'll try once more." He ruffled some papers, then picked up the phone and called the book bindery.

"Jesus spoke those words through me," Maria whispered to Mary. "I'd never have the courage to speak up to that man like that!"

The women could hear the little man sputtering. "But this woman is a good worker. She's all alone with a child to support, no unemployment or welfare. She left New York to live in our nice town, and how can we let her down?" He listened a moment. "Even if you did lay off the whole bunch, put this one back to work." His voice seemed urgent, almost insistent. "Put her to work doing anything. What do you want her to do? Starve?" There was another moment of silence, then, "You know we don't allow beggars in this town," he growled, "and she doesn't look like a beggar to me. She's a woman of faith!" He hung up the telephone and chuckled. Scribbling something on a yellow piece of paper, he handed it to Maria. The note read, "Go back to your job, Mrs. Diaz!"

Outside, Maria handed the note to Mary. Mary read it, then slipped an arm around Maria. Her voice choked. "I love you," she said quietly.

Still, at the book bindery Maria earned barely enough to live on. One day her antiquated refrigerator quit working. After examining it, the repairman concluded, "It's too old. There's no use repairing this thing even if I could." A few days later, Maria's twin bed broke and had to be hauled away with the refrigerator for junk. She pushed the two overstuffed chairs in her living room together (there was no couch), put the mattress on them, and made a bed for herself. "At least Dulcita's bed still holds up," she thought, and she thanked God that they still had a roof over their heads.

"Mommy," Dulcita said one morning as she sat at the breakfast table, "just look at those holes in the linoleum. Aren't we ever going to fix up anything around this apartment?"

The final blow came when Maria fell sick and was unable to work for more than a week. She flung the lumpy mattress from her broken bed onto the living room floor and tried to nurse herself back to health. She thought and prayed a lot during her illness, and she finally said, "Lord, I don't deserve anything on this earth because You have promised me eternal life and I am very happy. If You want to give me a bed and a few things You can see I need in this apartment I'll gladly accept them, but I leave that up to You. May Your will be done. Amen."

An idea came to her mind as she prayed. "Go see that wealthy relative of yours in New York." She knew he wasn't a Christian, nor did he always make good use of his money, yet she still hated to beg from him. She told the Lord how she felt, but the impression to go see her relative came on stronger than ever. "Perhaps I could help him find Jesus," she thought. She pulled herself up from the mattress and struggled into her clothes.

She had no money for train fare, but she acted on faith that God would provide a way to New York. She found a ride with a student from the college who was going home for a few days. They inched along in a blinding snowstorm, but "by faith the fellow got us to New York," she told Dulcita later.

Maria spent the night in the home of one of her brothers. The next morning her brother dropped her off at the hospital where her relative worked. The operator at the switchboard paged him, and she sat waiting for him in a chair in a basement hallway outside the lab. Sitting there she recalled a previous weekend when she had been a guest in this relative's home. Maria had noted the luxury throughout the entire house. His wife had treated Maria graciously, and she did not begrudge her relatives their comfortable living. But she realized that they had money to spare, and, to her knowledge, were not giving any of it to the Lord. "Now," she thought, "perhaps Jesus wants them to put some of it to good use in helping me."

"How are you, Maria?" the tall, dark-haired young man asked as he reached her side. "I'm so glad you came to see me here, because my wife is away from home right now."

"Angelo!" Maria smiled and shook his hand. "I'm fine, thank you," she murmured, "and you're looking well."

"Tell me. How are things in your home? And how are you managing financially?"

Maria's heart flipped. "God even furnished the opening line for me," she thought.

"Everything is really wonderful," she said. "The Lord is blessing me in a very special way, except that my bed broke and my refrigerator broke, but I am happy because Jesus is whole, and as long as Jesus doesn't break, everything is fine! Jesus will never end. He is infinite."

Angelo looked straight into Maria's face. "You've been sleeping on the floor, have you? And you have no refrigerator? Yet everything is 'just fine'? How long have you been living this way?"

"Quite a while now, and another thing. I've been sick. I haven't been able to work for quite a while."

"And you're happy, huh?"

"Sure I am," Maria replied. "Money is not everything."

Just then there was a commotion down the hall. Two young men swung a gurney out into the hall from a door marked Morgue and started toward them. A corpse lay on the gurney, all but its feet covered with a white sheet and an identification tag tied to one of its big toes. The boys joked and laughed as they passed by.

Angelo shook his head as the gurney passed them. "Did you see that, Maria? That's the way we're all going to go out of this world—feet first!" He sighed. "Now look at you. Look at how you have to live, and you still insist that you're happy? Maria, I don't understand you!"

"I've learned not to complain about my lot in life," Maria said. "It's part of being a Christian. I just take my problems to God, and He solves them for me."

Angelo's eyes took on a faraway look, as though his mind were trying to digest what Maria had said. Then, without another word, he took a checkbook from his pocket and began writing. A moment later he tore the check out and handed it to her.

Maria gasped. "One thousand dollars! It will take me forever to pay this back."

"If you can, fine. Don't worry though. Take care of yourself!"

"I could have done with second-hand furniture," she murmured.

"No! Use it to buy yourself something good for once. I want you to have a brand new bed and refrigerator. If you need more, let me know, and I will send it to you."

Tears sprang to Maria's eyes and rolled down her cheeks. Neither of them spoke for a minute. "Do you know why I'm crying?" she asked him at last. "It's because you haven't given your heart to Jesus. You freely gave me a thousand dollars. You could just as freely give Him your life, and that would mean more to Jesus and to me than all the money in the world."

He reached over and patted her hand. "Don't worry," he told her, "the time will come for me." He turned and brushed away a tear.

Angelo's time did come. Some months later Maria received a letter from him telling her that he had been baptized into the Seventh-day Adventist Church, "and you were the one who turned my thoughts in that direction," he wrote. "Thank you, Maria, God bless you."

Little Sister Helen

While living in Massachusetts, Maria occasionally visited New York to see her brothers and sisters, making it possible for Dulcita to visit her father also. On one such visit, they had not seen Henrique in over a year. As they stood on the front porch of the apartment house waiting for Henrique to answer their knock, Dulcita remarked, "Look at those pretty chrysanthemums blooming along the driveway, Mother. I don't remember seeing any flowers in the yard when I was here last time."

"Somebody has taken an interest in this yard," Maria replied.

A young, pregnant woman answered their knock. Maria assumed that she was the wife of the apartment owner. "May I help you?" she asked pleasantly.

"We're looking for Mr. Sanchez," Maria answered. "Does he still live here?"

"Oh, yes," the woman said. "Please come in." She led them to the parlor and offered them a seat. "I'll call Mr. Sanchez," she told them, and she climbed a stairway.

"Henrique had a ground-floor room before," Maria remarked.

"I know," Dulcita said, "but here comes Daddy now."

"What a pleasant surprise!" Henrique exclaimed as he hugged Dulcita warmly. The young woman who had opened the door followed Henrique into the living room.

As they all seated themselves, she sat beside him on the sofa, but he did not introduce her. Maria watched her while Dulcita and her father carried on a lively conversation. Finally Maria said, "I think we should be going, Dulcita. I still need to visit my niece while we're here in New York." To her surprise, Henrique offered to drive them over in his car.

"Who's that pregnant woman?" Maria asked after they left. Henrique did not answer. Maria rephrased her question, "Is that your wife, Henrique?"

"Yes," he replied. "As you can see, we are expecting an addition to our family in a few months, so we are buying that house." Unbeknown to Maria, following his three-day visit to them in Massachusetts when they could not reconcile their religious differences, Henrique had followed her advice to find a good woman and marry her.

Maria became very excited, "Oh, Dulcita, how beautiful! You're going to have a baby brother or sister! Let's go see that woman again. She was so sweet!" Henrique turned the car around.

Carmen was surprised to see her guests returning so soon and was more surprised when Maria hurried over and hugged her. "Oh, Carmen! How beautiful that you're going to have a baby."

Carmen's eyes radiated welcome. "Do you have to go home tonight? Can't you stay here with us?"

"Why not?" Maria said. "We can catch an early train in the morning."

With the help of her two guests, Carmen began cooking supper. She pointed to a bottle of oil on the counter. "I don't cook with lard," she said, assuring Maria that, as Adventists, they could eat her meal. Maria was surprised and quickly learned that while Carmen was not a practicing Christian, she had attended the Adventist church many times as a girl and was thoroughly acquainted with the church's teachings. "Praise the Lord! Praise the Lord!" Maria thought. "He has a plan yet for Henrique to be saved. I just know it now!" She and Carmen discussed the church while getting dinner, but Maria avoided pressing Carmen about her own spiritual life. Everyone sat around the dining-room table as though it happened every day, and Maria was overjoyed.

As they left the house the next morning Dulcita squeezed her father's hand and reminded him one last time, "Call us fast when the baby's born, Daddy! I want to come to New York then, as soon as I can, to see my new little brother or sister."

"Oh, the baby will be a girl, honey," Henrique laughed. "Don't you know that I'm partial to little girls?"

Maria and Dulcita didn't wait till the baby arrived to return though, because Maria wanted to stay especially close to them. Eventually she confided in Carmen, "I'm so glad that Henrique has found a wife to be happy with. He needed you. Do you know how I can be so happy, even though I live alone with my daughter?"

Carmen looked at the older woman. "No, tell me."

"At one time I did love Henrique very much. But we were not good for each other. Now, in place of a husband, I have a wonderful Friend. His name is Jesus."

"Oh," Carmen said. "I used to know Jesus a little better than I do now."

"I'll be praying for you to renew your friendship with Jesus," she said, and then she added, "especially for the baby's sake." Maria and Dulcita visited New York frequently, and before the baby was even born, Carmen and Henrique had decided, at Maria's suggestion, to have their baby dedicated in the Adventist church.

Finally the telephone call came. Henrique had been right. "It's a girl!" he announced proudly, "and we've named her Helen, only her nickname is Cookie because she is so sweet." He described the baby as best he could and ended by saying, "Come up as soon as you can to see your little sister, Dulcita."

A few days later Maria and Dulcita returned to New

York. Dulcita ran up the front steps of her father's house. "Baby Helen is beautiful!" she exclaimed as she stood over the bassinet.

"Go get your mother," Henrique and Carmen said at once.

Dulcita flew back out the front door and down the steps. "Mommy! Mommy! Come up! They want you to see the baby too."

The baby lay asleep in her bassinet. She had dark hair above rosy red cheeks, a rosebud mouth, and tiny fingers curled around the satin edge of the blanket. "Precious," Maria said.

"May I pick her up?" Dulcita looked at Carmen, then at her father.

"Go ahead," Henrique said. "She won't break."

Carmen leaned over and whispered in Maria's ear. "I had a hard time of it, and the doctor says I mustn't try again. So this will be it. No sons for Henrique."

"Do you think he's disappointed?" Maria asked.

"Oh, no. He claims he wanted another girl. We must keep the girls in touch with each other, though, since it will be so good each of them has a sister. As it turned out, all three parents were eager to foster a close relationship between the girls, and Henrique did his best to make it so. Every other month he and Carmen and Helen went to Massachusetts for a weekend, and the months between he sent Maria extra money for her and Dulcita to spend a weekend in New York. Each time they visited New York, Maria was allowed to bring the baby into the guest room with her for the night. Henrique and Carmen even consented for her to take the baby to church. Maria's one desire was that Cookie should learn to love Jesus.

Maria arranged to have baby Helen dedicated one Sabbath morning in the South Lancaster village church when Henrique and Carmen drove up from New York to spend the weekend. Henrique was still a spiritualist, but he was accepting Seventh-day Adventist ways. He told

Maria that if he ever came to be a member of any church, it would be the Seventh-day Adventist Church. "I know it's the right one," he told her. Maria knew that Henrique was a very good man. He had just grown up in the wrong atmosphere.

Christmas was a very special time. Each Christmas after Cookie was born, Maria and Dulcita would go to New York, and Henrique would have a lovely big tree decorated for his daughters. Dulcita was overjoyed to be able to have Christmas as one big family.

Carmen was happy too. "She is a very good woman," Maria thought. As baby Helen grew, she began pulling herself up on the furniture and soon she was toddling around. Both Dulcita and Maria enjoyed those visits, and Helen's parents seemed to enjoy sharing her.

When Helen grew a little older she liked nothing better than to visit her sister and Auntie Maria. She especially enjoyed Dulcita's teenage hat collection. She would first try on a Davy Crockett fur cap or a Daniel Boone coonskin cap with its tail swinging, and then a movie star's straw-brimmed picture hat with blue flowers draped on it, and another, and another. "See, Sissy?" she would say.

Then, just before Helen was old enough to start school, Henrique and Carmen decided to move back to Puerto Rico. The two sisters, bidding each other tearful good-byes, were to be separated for several years.

Wedding Bells

A student had just arrived from Germany to enroll for the second semester when school opened at Atlantic Union College after the Christmas holiday early in 1961. In addition to whatever deeper qualities he possessed, Gerhard Steinbacher was the tall, dark, and handsome prince that rides into every girl's dreams.

His first Friday night on campus a teacher befriended him and accompanied him to the evening meeting, and they sat on the right side of the chapel.

Gerhard kept looking toward the left, watching the girls come in. "That one's rather pretty," he said, leaning over and whispering to his new friend. "There's another pretty one." This continued until Dulcita came in. And that was the end of Gerhard's girl watching. Gerhard's eyes followed Dulcita to her seat and never left her all evening.

Monday Gerhard walked into his English class, and there was Dulcita! He chose a seat close to her and asked her if she could help him with his English. Dulcita thought this was a logical request from someone recently arrived from another country who had somewhat of a language problem. After class Gerhard accompanied Dulcita to the post office, which happened to be across the street from her apartment. She pointed out her house to him and bade him goodbye.

"Mamma, Mamma, I just met the most wonderful fellow!" Dulcita exclaimed as she burst into the apartment a few minutes later. She talked of little else the rest of the day. Dulcita never dated anyone else after that. She introduced him to Maria as Gary, the American name she gave him.

After graduation they were married in the South Lancaster village Seventh-day Adventist church. Henrique and Carmen came from Puerto Rico to attend the wedding. When the family and wedding party returned to Maria's home for dinner after the rehearsal, Henrique began to weep. He felt guilty about the past and wished he could have been with Dulcita when she was growing up. Turning to Maria, he said sadly, "And now you are going to be all alone." Dulcita began to cry too.

Maria stood up. "This is a happy day! What are we crying for? I prayed all my life that I would live to see Dulcita march down two aisles, one on her graduation day and again on her wedding day to a good man. I have lived to see this day! Forget the past. Live for the beautiful times ahead! And don't worry about me. Jesus has always been with me. I have Him, and He is more than anybody else!" Everyone applauded when she sat down.

Henrique was very touched by the ceremony itself, especially as he walked his daughter down the aisle to become Mrs. Gary Steinbacher. The minister asked, "Who giveth this woman away?"

"Her mother and I," Henrique said, and he broke down and cried softly.

In spite of Maria's brave words at the rehearsal dinner, it was very hard for her to see Dulcita's room empty. After Dulcita and Gary left for a Niagara Falls honeymoon, Maria felt that they had gone forever.

Following their honeymoon, Gary and Dulcita moved to Blue Mountain Academy in Pennsylvania, where he taught German and French and Dulcita taught home economics. Maria quickly learned to love Gary as her own son, and he and their two sons, Michael and Leroy, hold the same place as Dulcita in Maria's heart.

After Dulcita and Gary's wedding, Helen, now ten, returned to Puerto Rico with her parents. A few years later a large Seventh-day Adventist evangelistic crusade was held, and Henrique was touched that the evangelist and his wife visited them in their home. "These people are really nice to do this," he told Carmen, and he began accepting Bible studies from them for his family. Several months later he accepted the minister's invitation to join Carmen and Helen and 100 other candidates who were baptized in the ocean one Sabbath day.

Teresa's Stars for Maria's Crown

Even before Dulcita's wedding, Maria's heart began reaching out to Teresa's children. Their mother had suffered poor health for several years. The mushrooming cancer finally smothered Teresa's life. One of the four children she left behind was Luis.

Little Luey always had been close to Aunt Maria, especially since the day in Puerto Rico, before Maria's conversion, when she had spanked him for waking her up early at 6:00 a.m. Luey, only a little over two at the time, had sat in his highchair with the tears rolling down his cheeks singing "Happy day, O happy day . . . when Jesus washed my sins away."

Maria had quickly repented of her senseless anger and snuggled the innocent toddler in her arms. How could he know that at that early hour Aunt Maria needed her sleep?

"Sorry, baby, Auntie Maria shouldn't have done that," she said, and tears began to roll down her cheeks too.

He threw his chubby little arms around her neck as he told her, "Don't cwy, Auntie. Don't cwy."

Luey was always a special child to his Aunt Maria. A strong love bond had existed between them from that day forward. Maria longed to be as patient as her sister. With her fierce denunciation years before of Teresa's religion, Maria herself had contributed much to the development of Teresa's patience. She wondered, after her conversion, how she could ever redeem the years of misery that she had caused her sister. Now, with Teresa dead, Maria took the two motherless boys, Reuben, eleven, and Luis, ten, with her to Massachusetts as her own.

Reuben was a good boy when he lived with Maria—very obedient and helpful around the house. But he seemed troubled and distant. "If God loves Luey and me, why did He let our mother die?" he would ask. His boyish mind seemed to reject all Maria's explanations. "We needed her," he insisted. "Didn't God know that?" In spite of all Maria could do or say, Reuben seemed to be drawing away from God and rejecting his mother's religion. He never enjoyed religion the way Luey did.

Luey especially loved singing. The veins in his neck bulged as he sang, "I am so glad that Jesus loves me." Maria wondered that his little throat could take it and felt that he would surely swallow his vocal cords. During worship the boy loved to sing and pantomime the songs.

Luey wanted to be a minister. From early childhood, while his mother still lived, he told her that someday he would preach sermons like their minister, whom he adored. As Maria watched, Luey would call his playmates together and lead song service under the trees in the yard. Then he would stand on a stump and preach to them. The boys and girls listened with rapt attention. He even passed the offering plate, collecting stones, and dismissed the meeting with a little prayer.

Occasionally, Luey would lose his temper, and his playmates would tease him. "Luey, you can't be a preacher. You get mad too easy," they would say. Then Luey would feel sorry and ask their forgiveness.

"You can be a *good* minister, Luey," Aunt Maria would tell him when he came inside the house. "As long as you are sorry for your sins, God can use you. I expect to hear you preach powerful sermons in a real church someday."

"Yes," he would say, "that's what I'm going to be when I grow up!"

When Luey was eleven, Reuben went back to New York to stay with his father. Maria felt sad to see him go, but she felt even worse when a letter came from Pedro. "I am coming to get Luis next Sunday," he wrote. "The boys need to be together, and Reuben will suffer if Luis stays."

"Why, oh why, should a child who loves religion have to be taken from it?" Maria asked herself over and over.

"I don't want to leave here," Luey kept telling her. "Please let me stay with you, Aunt Maria."

Maria hugged him and promised to pray about it. "But if your father said you must go, only God could change that," she warned.

"I'll pray too," Luey promised, and he did, every morning and evening all that week.

On Friday afternoon Luey climbed up onto the roof of the house to help a repairman fix a leak. Maria heard him singing his favorite song at the top of his voice: "I am so glad that Jesus loves me."

It nearly tore Maria's heart out. "Please, Lord, do *something* about this," she pleaded. "That boy wants to serve You. He is such a good boy, such a Christian! He wants to be a minister."

Luey was to leave on Sunday. Saturday night Maria took Luey to vespers with her, and afterward they stopped at the post office. There was a letter from Pedro. Maria tore it open and read it to Luey. "I've decided not to bring Luey to New York just now. I know he would suffer. He likes religion, and I don't like religion. You keep him, Maria."

"Glory be!" shouted Maria, and Luey began to sing, "I am so glad. . . ."

As he grew into his teenage years, Luey decided to visit his father and brother and the city again. He packed his suitcase and caught a bus to New York. Maria missed him, and she always remembered to pray for him three times a day.

One evening three years later, Maria heard a knock on the door. "I came to visit you, Aunt Maria," he said, and he put an arm around her and kissed her. Luey arrived during Friday night worship, and he joined her in singing.

"What sweet memories you bring me tonight," Maria said after they had prayed.

"It reminds me of when I lived with you and we had worship every day," he said. "But Friday night worship was always so special." Maria sensed a longing in his voice.

Luey stayed about an hour and then went to see his sister, Olga, who lived in the next town. Maria kept praying for him. The next Friday evening about worshiptime Luey appeared again, this time with a suitcase in his hand! "You came to spend the night!" Maria cried.

"I came to stay," Luey said, and he moved into his old room.

Maria hadn't said anything to persuade Luey. She knew that the Holy Spirit had worked on his heart and that "her boy" had come back, not only to her, but to Jesus as well, for he told her he was going to prepare himself for baptism. Since he had dropped out of school to work, Maria urged him to go to Union Springs Academy in upstate New York and finish high school. Luey realized that if he were ever to realize his dream of becoming a minister, he would have to finish his education. "Union Springs Academy would work out fine for me, Aunt Maria," he agreed. "There's a special minister friend of mine up there, and I'd like for him to baptize me."

Maria's heart sang with joy. "You'll be the best singing evangelist in New England," she told him with pride.

Luey worked all summer and saved his money. In the fall he had enough for his entrance fee and a little left over. Because he was older than most of the boys, the dean chose him to be his assistant. By selling Christian books in the summer and assisting the dean in the winter, Luey was able to earn his way through two years of academy.

When Luey graduated, Aunt Maria was on the front row and afterward was the first person to reach his side to congratulate him. After a kiss and a hug and a picture or two, he leaned over and whispered, "I'm thinking of studying business. What do you think of that?"

"But I thought you wanted to be a minister?" Maria showed her disappointment. Then she brightened, "Why not take both theology and business together?"

"That would be a good idea," he said. "That way if I cannot be a minister, I can be a good businessman in one of our academies."

Four years later Luey graduated from Atlantic Union College with a major in theology and a minor in business. Again Maria was present, and again she shed tears for both Teresa and herself. A few months later Luis enrolled at Andrews University to study for his master of divinity degree.

In addition to Luey and Reuben, Maria also took in Madeline, the thirteen-year-old daughter of her brother, Santos. Santos had recently divorced his wife and wanted Madeline to enjoy the same childhood environment, out of New York, that Dulcita had had.

Within a year, Maria's prayers influenced Madeline to ask if she could be baptized. Madeline finished academy and attended Atlantic Union College for one year. But she met a fine Christian young man—Kurt Durrschmedt—married him, and quit school. Soon three lovely children joined the family.

Suddenly, tragedy struck that home. Madeline suffered from severe headaches that could not be diagnosed. One day, without warning, she discovered that she could not see, and within half an hour was completely paralyzed. Kurt rushed her to the hospital, where a neurologist examined her and operated that night, removing a cancerous brain tumor. Still the headaches persisted. Several months later tests showed that she suffered from an inoperable brain tumor.

Maria visited Madeline in the hospital. She held her hand and prayed for her. "Madeline's beauty is still stunning," she wrote to Dulcita the next day. "Her wavy brown hair covers her head as it rests silently on the pillow under the resuscitator. It seems impossible to Kurt and me that we are going to lose her."

At Madeline's funeral both of her parents expressed their gratitude to Maria for what she had done to help their daughter in her growing-up years. "The only thing we can be sure of," they said, "is that Madeline died saved."

Raising Up a Church

One day Maria received a phone call from Dulcita. "Gary and I are moving to Connecticut so he can work on his Ph.D. We are wondering whether you could come and live with us and take care of the boys while Gary studies and I work."

If Maria's cherished family needed her, that is where she would be. She packed up and moved to Connecticut. Now Maria lived in the country. Since she did not drive, she could not reach people to share Jesus. In the past, colporteuring had taken her from house to house to meet people. But now, as after her baptism, she became depressed and sad.

"How can I be happy when I can't win souls?" she said to Dulcita. "Only one more. Only one more!"

One day she felt impressed to pick up the telephone book. She skimmed through, looking for Spanish surnames. Presently, however, she came across the name of an Adventist pastor. She called and told him just how she felt.

"I'm so glad you called," he said. "We have many Spanish people in our town! We welcome you to our church and would be most happy to have you begin a Spanish service!" That was all Maria needed to hear. Every Sabbath afternoon she and three other Spanish members went out to visit Spanish people and invite them to church. Maria was in charge of the service, and soon it had to be moved to a gymnasium for more room.

One day she told the Lord, "I don't want to wait for Sabbath afternoon to go out. I want a soul *today!* I'm in great need of one today. Please show me where I can find one. Thank You. Amen." Right away it came to her mind that she should go to the school where Dulcita taught English to Spanish-speaking residents. She boarded a bus.

At the school a half hour later, she looked over the class. "I know there's a soul in here. The Lord told me there is," she said to herself. "All I need to do is figure out which one it is." Dulcita introduced her mother to the class.

It happened that a birthday party was going on for one of the students. After the games, when it was time to sit down, there was no chair for Maria. One of the students, Vicente Crespo, brought her a chair. He had dark hair, a fair complexion, and a fresh smile. Maria knew at once that this was her "soul"! She learned that his parents lived in Puerto Rico and that he lived with his brother in Connecticut.

"I'm going to have a birthday soon," Maria said. "Do you want to come to my party?"

"When is your birthday?" Vicente asked.

"This coming Sabbath. Can you come?"

He sat back. "Sure I will come," he said with a smile. "What do you like for a present?"

"I would be happy to receive a present from you," Maria replied. "Maybe you won't want to give me the kind of present I am going to ask you for, but maybe you will!"

"Whatever you want, Mrs. Diaz, I will give it to you!"

Maria liked him. It was so beautiful to hear a young person talk like that. "I go to the Seventh-day Adventist church," she said. "I am a member there. Do you know about the Seventh-day Adventist church?"

"Oh, yes, yes! I know who the Seventh-day Adventists are!"

Maria told him where the church was located. "Sabbath morning we have a Sabbath School first, and I am in charge," she said. "I am going to ask you to come to my service—for me. All I want for my birthday is to see you there. That will be the biggest present you can give me."

"Mrs. Diaz, I am sorry, but what you are asking me I will not be able to give you," he answered.

"Oh, you cannot?" Maria asked sadly.

"I will give you something else," he said.

"I don't need anything else. I have everything I need besides that one present," Maria told him. The boy became nervous. "Why can't you do it?" she asked.

"I am a very strict Catholic. I am an altar boy, and I cannot go to other churches."

"Oh, I'm sorry. You don't have to give me the present if you can't. But don't worry about it, we can always be friends anyway. I love you; you know that," Maria said. Maria went home and began praying for Vicente even though she set aside any idea of his coming to church.

But, Sabbath morning as she was going up to the platform, she found him sitting on the front row! He stood when he saw her, walked along with her a few steps, and took her hand. "Here is the present for your birthday, Mrs. Diaz," he said.

"Thank you! Thank you very much!" There were tears in Maria's eyes. "Thank You so much, God, for my one soul," she whispered. A few minutes later Maria asked Vicente to stand, and she introduced him to the congregation. Vicente looked all around and smiled, and after the service the young people surrounded him and gave him a Bible. He stayed all day, first for the potluck dinner, then for the literature distribution in the afternoon, and finally for vespers at sundown. He even stayed for the pizza social that evening. A few months later Vicente was baptized, and Maria thanked God for her "one soul."

Vicente's brother, however, could not accept Vicente's new convictions on diet and health. He made life difficult for Vicente, especially for not eating pork. Finally, Vicente returned home to Puerto Rico. Some time later, Adventist evangelistic meetings were being held in Maria's city. She was standing at the door, passing out literature, when a young man walked up to her.

"Are you Mrs. Diaz?"

"Yes."

"My name is Salvadore," he said, "and I am here because Vicente talked so much about you."

"Oh," Maria thought, "here comes the other one!" "That is wonderful!" she said. "I miss Vicente so much, and now you will take his place."

"Yes, I think so," he said. Tears came to his eyes as he told Maria how bad he felt for having given Vicente such a hard time.

Eventually Salvadore was baptized, along with five other people he brought with him. Among them were his girlfriend and her mother.

After returning home, Vicente studied theology for two years at Antillian Adventist College and is now a Christian worker in Puerto Rico, married, with two children. "I'm so glad I found you," he wrote to Maria. "I pray to the Lord with tears in my eyes all the time to be with you. I'm going to buy a horse to go to the mountains and the places where cars cannot go, and do missionary work." Another letter said, "Tomorrow will be a baptism, and many, many 'grandchildren' of yours will be baptized. You don't know, sister dear, how happy I am in the Lord. I'm so grateful to God for sending you to me."

After three years in Connecticut, Dulcita and Gary moved to Michigan to teach at Andrews University, and Maria went with them. During her stay in Connecticut Maria had been instrumental in raising up a church which, by the time she left, numbered 150 members. Membership today stands at more than 300—all because Maria begged the Lord for "one more soul, just one more soul!"

Maria's "Love Children"

Mr. Garber, the business manager at Andrews University, had given Maria almost no encouragement the morning she appeared in his office to ask for work. "I'm sorry," he told her, "but the students come first, and I have given all the work there is to them."

With a smile Maria handed him a slip of paper on which she had written her name and telephone number. "Please call me," she said. "I will be waiting."

Although his eyes registered sympathy, he shook his head. "I wouldn't count on it," he cautioned. "There are more students asking for work all the time. I have to turn some of them away or give them work they don't like. Usually, they'll even take that, they are so desperate to stay in school."

Maria sighed. She had just come from Connecticut to Michigan. She had only $600 to her name, and she felt that she had to have work. But then she said, again with a smile, "I have faith to believe that God will give me work."

At home she told Dulcita, "God knows I have to have work, so I'm not going to worry about it." But she called Mr. Garber's office frequently to ask if any jobs had become available.

"Maria," he said on one occasion when she called, and his voice came over the wire kindly, "if you had more education—if you were a teacher or a librarian or asking for anything besides a cleaning job, perhaps I could find something for you. But with no more education than you have had, it just looks impossible."

"Thank you, Mr. Garber. But I still believe Jesus will find some work for me." Maria's faith never faltered.

"You don't need to worry, Mother," Dulcita assured her. "You are welcome in my home as long as you want to stay."

"I know. But I can't be happy without working and paying my own way," Maria replied. And she kept on praying.

Maria hummed a tune as she washed the breakfast dishes one morning after Dulcita had left for her work. She felt unusually happy because she had decided that if Jesus brought her to Michigan, He would give her work. This particular morning she felt "for sure" that work would come her way. Maybe even that day.

The telephone rang. Maria answered it, and she immediately recognized Mr. Garber's voice. "I want you to come to my office as soon as you can." He hesitated, then went on. "One of the two cleaning ladies at the men's dormitory—Meier Hall—has taken ill and needs surgery. She'll have to give up her job. Can you come this morning?"

"Sure, I can," Maria responded promptly. "I'll be there in half an hour." Drying her hands, she brushed her hair and slipped on a clean dress. Walking across campus to Mr. Garber's office she almost felt as though she was floating on a cloud. He explained that she would be directing the boys who did the janitorial work. She was responsible to see that every nook and corner of her half of the dormitory sparkled when the work was done. Maria's smile spread from ear to ear. "That work I like, Mr. Garber. Thank you. Thank you."

Mr. Garber held up his hand. "Don't thank me. I really thought there would be no job for you on this campus, Maria, but I see that God has provided one."

"Yes," Maria agreed, and she headed for Meier Hall.

Maria enjoyed her new job. By the time she had worked there a month she realized that her real mission in Meier Hall was to be an "undercover agent" for God. What better place could she find to be a missionary than a dormitory full of homesick boys eager to adopt a second mom?

Steve's friendly brown eyes searched Maria out every morning before he rushed off to his classes. An eighteen-year-old freshman, he was always neatly dressed, his straight brown hair brushed into place, his shoes polished. "Such a decent, refined young man," Maria thought. They loved to talk together, sharing their experiences with Jesus. Sometimes they prayed together, and in his prayers he always mentioned his father and mother, who were considering a divorce. Maria heard tears in his voice as he pleaded with God to save his parents' marriage.

But one morning Steve rushed past her as he bounded down the stairs, brushing her arm, but not stopping to look at her or speak.

"That's just not like Steve," Maria thought. She turned and called after him. No answer. She ran after him, thinking, "Something is wrong with that boy. I can't let him go out the door like this." She called, but Steve only walked faster and refused to answer.

Maria stopped in her tracks and began to pray. Steve, too, stood still, his hand on the outside door. Maria ran to him. "Steve," she cried, "what's wrong? Please listen to me." She laid a hand on his arm. He shook it off and turned away from her. She walked around in front of him and saw that his eyes were red from crying.

"Leave me alone, Maria." He whispered so that others would not hear.

"Whatever is the matter with you, Steve? You know that I love you. Please tell me what's wrong." She held his arm with her hand.

"Don't bother me!" he exploded. "I have to go someplace."

"You can go where you have to go, but talk to me first."

"No, I haven't time. Let me go." He jerked away, and Maria noticed that his brown eyes swam in tears.

She lowered her voice. "Steve," she said, "whatever bothers you is getting to me too. This morning I felt so depressed. I need to talk to you. You are my friend, and I don't have another friend like you. Please, Steve, I need you!"

Steve gave Maria a strange look. Gently, she coaxed him back to his room. When he had closed the door he blurted out, "Well, then, talk to me. What do you want? Hurry up, because I have to go someplace, and I am already late."

"I want to pray with you," Maria said.

"You pray all you want, but leave me out of it." His voice was rough. Maria called to Jesus, "Please come to Steve and me right in this room, Jesus. Something's wrong with both of us, and we don't know what it is. But I do know that all we need is You. Please come close to us, dear Lord. Wrap us in Your love."

Steve began to sob, and his tense body shook all over. Maria put her hand on his shoulder and let him cry; then she held him in her arms while he cried. "I guess . . . I won't go . . . where I was going after all," he said at last.

"Where were you going, Steve? Could I go for you?" Maria asked.

Steve's head jerked up. "No!" he cried. "No, never! I hope you never want to go where I was going when you stopped me."

"Where were you going, Steve?" Maria's voice sounded gentle, but in her heart she feared what he would answer.

"I was going down to the St. Joseph River to drown myself. My parents are going through with the divorce in spite of all my prayers. Mom told me on the phone this morning that I must choose which one of them I want to live with." He broke down again, then recovered. "Mom said my little sister would stay with her, and if I wanted to, I could go with Dad. I guess I thought—well, I don't know. I thought if I did away with myself, then they wouldn't have to worry about whom I'd choose to live with." He paused, and a moment later a smile broke out across his tear-stained face. "That was silly, I suppose."

He relaxed and looked at Maria. "I'm going to call you 'Mamacita,' " he said gently. "My Spanish book tells me that means 'little mother' or 'sweetest mother' in Spanish."

"I'd like that," Maria said softly. "And, Steve, remember, Jesus and I love you, and we always will."

"Thanks," he said, looking in the mirror and brushing his hair into place with his fingers. "And now I'd better hurry to my first class. Thanks, Maria. I'll never forget this."

Maria became so involved in counseling "her boys" that she could not get her work done properly. One day she received a letter from her work supervisor demanding that she stop talking to the young men in the dormitory and pay attention to her work. A copy had been sent to the academic dean.

Maria fled to the dean's office. "I can't stop helping my boys," she pleaded. "I will work longer hours—anything to keep my job."

The dean looked at her kindly. "I don't think your supervisor understands the good work you are doing, Maria," he said. "I know what you are doing because the boys tell me about it when they come in here. You are doing something that needs to be done on this campus, and no one else is doing it. Go home and rest a few days. I'll see what I can work out."

Maria went home and prayed. The next day she received a phone call from the vice-president's office. Could she report there in two hours?

The dean and the new labor director were also waiting in the office when she entered. The men stood and offered her a chair, and then they sat down. The vice-president said, "We've heard excellent reports about your counseling in Meier Hall, my dear lady. The way we see it, we have you doing the right work, but in the wrong place. We have another job for your consideration, where you'll be able to help both the young men and the young women on this campus. How would you like to be the hostess in the Campus Center Student Lounge?"

For a moment Maria could not speak. No more cleaning! No more hurrying the boys at their work! Plenty of time to talk with them, pray with them, mother them! She felt absolutely elated, but she answered simply, "Yes, I would like that!"

Maria's "Hot Line" to Heaven

Maria sat in front of a large desk and supervised the activities in the student lounge. Her heart thrilled as she watched the young people come and go, some in groups, some two-by-two. When they saw the new hostess, many of them stopped by to get acquainted with her. Others carried on lively conversations interspersed with laughter. All of them seemed relaxed in the restful atmosphere.

Sometimes a couple came to sit on one of the sofas, holding hands and looking into each other's eyes—"serious, very much in love," Maria thought. Were they planning next summer's wedding or discussing their future together? Maria's romantic heart loved these couples, and she felt pleased that they had a safe place to enjoy each other's company.

But trouble drifted into the lounge the very first Sabbath she spent on duty. A group of black students had gathered in the south end of the large room while a group of white students assembled in the north end. Threatening glances passed between the two groups.

"The old devil is at work," Maria said to herself, and she watched the two groups of young people with growing concern. She didn't recognize having seen any of them in the lounge before, but she felt the tension building up. The blacks began shouting taunts, and the white students shouted them back. Maria knew the black young people had recently experienced the assassination of Martin Luther King, Jr. The thought crossed her mind that she could not handle this job. "But God can handle it," she said to herself. "Lord, what am I to do?"

She noticed angry looks coming her way from both groups, and she realized that they expected her to do something. But what? She knew that she must pray alone, so she headed for the ladies' restroom nearby.

An angry white student blocked her way. "Are you going to do something about this?" he demanded. His blue eyes flashed. He pushed his auburn hair out of his freckled face and blocked her way.

Maria tried to sound calm. "Don't worry. Something will be done. Just be patient. Go take a walk if you don't like this; then come back in a few minutes."

The young man stepped aside, still frowning.

"He probably thinks I don't know what to do," she thought, "and he's right. But Jesus knows, and I am going to call Him right now."

Maria threw herself on the sofa in the women's lounge. "Lord, I really don't know what to do with the explosive situation out there," she said. "Please, I need Your help. I can do so little without You, and I am so lonely." Maria began to cry. She cried for a few minutes, praying all the time. "I'm claiming Your promise to send the Holy Spirit. That's what we need. The antagonism out there is so strong, and I don't know what to do, Lord."

Maria spent nearly fifteen minutes talking to the Lord, hoping all the while that no blows had fallen out in the lounge. Finally she felt filled with the Holy Spirit and prepared to do what she had to do. "I'm not going out alone, Jesus," she whispered. "You are going with me, by my side."

And she heard Him say, "Have no fear; I am with you. Go. I will tell you what to do and say."

Maria reentered the lounge quietly, without fear. She walked over to the group of about fifty black students.

Since she didn't feel impressed to say anything, she stooped and began picking up the trash and pieces of fruit they had thrown on the floor. She arranged the furniture they had pushed around, putting it in order again. As she looked into their scowling faces she read insecurity mixed with anger, and her heart reached out to them. A feeling of love for them swept over her. She began to sing a hymn. The students quieted.

Maria said, "Hi. My name is Maria. I'm new here. This is my first Sabbath working in the student lounge. I'd like to know you better, so would you do me a favor?"

Silence. Maria continued, "I'm lonely. I don't have a single friend here—not one. But it's so beautiful to think you are all my brothers and sisters in Jesus. Thinking of Jesus makes me know I love you, even though I don't know you." She hesitated. They watched her. "I wish you would do me a favor," she repeated. "It would make me so happy." She waited.

Gradually their faces began to change. They weren't so hard now. Finally one girl snapped, "What?"

"You know, I would like to hear all of you singing. It would be so nice to hear you singing on the Sabbath day. Again I say, I am so lonely, and I would like you to be my brothers and sisters. I need you."

"Where you from?" asked a tall black boy with bushy hair.

"Puerto Rico," Maria said, smiling at him. "I speak Spanish better than I do English."

A black girl with ribbons in her hair began to hum a song; then she broke out singing in Spanish and the others joined her, one by one.

There were tears in Maria's eyes when the song ended. "You are so beautiful to me," she said.

They sang another song in Spanish, and a few white students drifted over. Soon the entire group of whites came over and they "mixed up," as Maria told it. A white theology student began talking about love—the love of

Jesus for each of them and how Christ wanted them all to love one another. A black student said Amen, and several on either side echoed him.

"Oh, do you know what is happening in this student lounge?" Maria asked. "There was one black Jesus and there was one white Jesus, but now there is only one Jesus—and nobody knows what color He is. We don't know how to love each other the way He tells us we should. And by not loving—well, sometimes we think about being saved and going to heaven. But how can we do that when everything we do here is full of hate and strong talk?" Several students dropped their eyes. Others murmured an Amen, and then a black boy began to pray.

A free-flowing prayer and testimony meeting followed. It continued from two o'clock in the afternoon until nearly six, and then it was time to stop for supper. A white boy suggested, "Let's sing, 'Blest Be the Tie that Binds,' " and they all began to join hands. Maria looked down and saw the white and black hands clasped, and tears flowed down her cheeks.

"Praise the Lord!" she cried. "Praise the Lord! The glory be for my God! Now I have many friends. Thank you, everyone, and God bless you," she murmured as the song ended.

Maria now understood that God had placed her in the student lounge to do a work for Him. She felt happy and secure, confident that Jesus would help her through any crisis. Black students who hadn't been in the group that Sabbath kept coming to her as if they knew her.

"Amy told me about you," one girl told her. "She says that you love us blacks."

"I had to get acquainted with you, Maria," another said. "About a dozen of my friends said you'd want to meet me."

And so the story spread. Both black and white students came seeking Maria as a friend, laughing with her, praying with her, and bringing new friends to get acquainted. Maria felt completely happy.

One day as Maria talked casually with an older student, a pretty black girl slipped up behind her and covered her eyes. "Guess who? Guess who?" she teased. Maria wrestled to turn around, and then she squealed, "Judi! Judi! How did you get here?"

"I was just driving through and thought I'd stop and see you," Judi answered. They hugged each other and talked for a few minutes. As Judi left she smiled at the older student. "A person never forgets his true friends," she said; then she skipped out.

"I must tell you about Judi," Maria said to the older girl. She explained that Judi used to come into the lounge with thunderclouds all over her face. She looked as if she hated everyone. She told Maria that she didn't like Andrews University, that her parents made her attend, and that she especially hated all the white students. But she didn't have any friends among the black students either, and Maria could tell that she was miserable. Nobody liked her. She talked too loud and tried to get others to say things against the school, the teachers, and the white students. She ignored all Maria's requests to keep her voice down.

"What shall I do with this Judi?" Maria would ask herself. She talked to Jesus, and one day He told her to walk over around Judi's chair and pick up some papers strewn on the floor. As she did, she hummed a little tune, and then came up behind Judi and laid a hand on her shoulder. Judi jumped back, startled. "Don't be afraid," Maria said. "It's only me." Then she said what Jesus told her to say: "How come you never smile?" Judi just looked at Maria with a solemn face, so Maria added, "You never come to me and say Hi like the rest of the students do. Come on, Judi, smile!"

Judi gave Maria a half smile, and Maria persisted, "Smile, Judi. I want to see a real smile on your beautiful face." Then Judi gave it to her, a charming smile with twinkling eyes, and from then on they became friends.

Judi began stopping by Maria's desk and asking her to tell stories about her life in Puerto Rico. On graduation day Judi kissed Maria and said, "I will miss you so much," and from then on, any time she was near the university she stopped to surprise her friend.

Maria's Healing Ministry

One day Maria spotted another student who never smiled. Kevin would walk by Maria's desk, nod, and speak, but an air of sadness hovered over him that bothered her. She prayed about Kevin as she worked, and then one day he seemed ready to talk. "Could we go into the faculty lounge where it's more private?" he asked. "I'd like to talk to you."

Maria's heart sang as she followed him into the room. During the few seconds it took to find a place to sit, she prayed for wisdom to help this troubled student. Kevin's wavy blonde hair fell across his long thin fingers, as he buried his face in his hands. For a few minutes he could not speak. Maria waited and prayed. Finally he raised his head and looked at her.

"I don't love my wife anymore," he blurted. "What am I going to do?" He brushed away some tears. "Last night I moved out on her. I just couldn't stand her anymore."

By gentle questioning, Maria learned that Kevin and Jennifer had married young, that she had given up getting an education in favor of being a good homemaker, and now Kevin would graduate with a degree in theology in the spring. "But how can I be a minister when I don't love my wife?" he asked, his voice barely a whisper.

Maria looked into his face a moment. "You have been fooling around with your eyes, haven't you, Kevin?

You've seen some other girls who look more interesting to you."

"How did you know?" he gasped.

"Oh, I've watched you in this student lounge. You haven't been physically untrue to your wife, but you know what the Bible says, Kevin. I don't have to tell you."

"I guess you've hit the nail on the head," Kevin admitted, lowering his eyes.

"If you think about other girls and imagine what it would be like to have one of them as your wife—" she paused. "You know what Jesus said about that, don't you?"

Kevin nodded.

"And, speaking of Jesus, how do you feel about Him?"

Kevin admitted that he had neglected his daily prayer and Bible study, so he felt far away from Jesus.

"You are going to mess up your entire life, Kevin," Maria warned. "The devil is after you. Don't let him do this to you. God has called you to the ministry, and Satan would like nothing better than to discourage you and lead you into sin. But God loves you and will help you through this trouble if you will let Him."

Kevin sat for a long time thinking. "I *could* love Jennifer," he said finally, "but I just wish she'd lay low for a while. It broke her heart when I moved out, but I didn't feel anything. I just didn't care. How could I be that way?"

"Your wife doesn't have anyone else to turn to. You are the one who's wrong, Kevin. Would you mind if I talked with Jennifer?"

"No, go right ahead." He seemed almost eager about the idea and gave Maria her address and phone number. Maria prayed with Kevin, and as soon as she finished work that afternoon, she went to Jennifer's apartment.

"Kevin agreed he needed a closer walk with Christ," Maria thought as she rang the doorbell. "Probably Jennifer needs that too. I'll try to bring the talk around to what is really lacking in their marriage."

A pretty blond girl answered the door. She was wearing a bright blue housecoat, and she looked at Maria with swollen eyes.

"Poor girl, she's been crying too," Maria thought. Then she spoke to the girl. "Hi, my name is Maria Diaz. I am the hostess at the campus student center, and I came to talk to you about Kevin."

The girl gasped. "Oh! How is he?" The eagerness in her face almost shocked Maria. She swung the door open wide. "Please come in, please come in!"

"He's all right," Maria said after they were seated in the small living room, "only he has wandered too far from Jesus."

Jennifer nodded. "We both did," she said. "We were so in love that we forgot to have worship or study and pray together until things began to go wrong. Then when I suggested to Kevin that we read our Bibles and pray together, he brushed me off, saying he had too much studying to do." Jennifer fought back the tears.

"Jennifer," Maria leaned over and took her hand and patted it. "Your apartment is very attractive. I can see that you work hard keeping it neat and clean. That helps. But there's one important thing about holding a husband. Unless Jesus lives in your family there can be no happiness or peace there."

Tears began running down Jennifer's cheeks. "I know. I know. How do I get him to come back so that we can invite Jesus in and try again to make our marriage work?"

"I'm going to ask you to do three things, Jennifer," Maria said. "First, pray for Kevin. Second, be faithful to him. Third, don't even consider a divorce. There's a fourth thing, and that may be the hardest of all to make yourself do. Find yourself a job, or if you have the funds, start back to school. You have to grow alongside your husband. You have to make a life for yourself. You mustn't cling to Kevin so tightly. You're strangling him. Do you see that?"

"I think I understand what you mean," Jennifer admitted. "I'll try what you have told me to do."

And she did. When Jennifer stopped depending on him for her only companionship, started taking a few classes and made new friends, Kevin moved back home.

"Moving out on Jennifer was my worst mistake," Kevin told Maria, "and yet God taught me a lesson I will never forget. I might have lost the sweetest wife in the world."

A year later Kevin accepted a call to be the assistant pastor of a church on the West Coast, with a special ministry in family life. When a baby girl joined their family their joy reached a new high. "We are so much in love," Kevin told Maria just before they left for the West Coast. "It's hard to believe those dark days ever happened."

One Indian summer day when the lounge stood deserted, a cocky young fellow pushed open the door and flopped on a bench. He wore shorts and a tank top. Maria watched him a few minutes, then drifted toward him, and in the kindest tone she could muster, she said, "You know you're not allowed in the campus center in those clothes." He gave her a belligerent look, but no answer. Neither did he move. Maria returned to her desk and prayed. When she approached him the second time, the boy stood up and faced her, a scornful look spread across his face.

"Do you think I'd leave this lousy place just because I am wearing shorts?" he challenged. "I won't. So what are you gonna do about that?"

Sadly, Maria shook her head. "I don't want to, but I will have to call security," she told him.

"Go ahead. Call security," he barked. "Call the whole university. Call anybody you want. I'm fed up with this whole business. I'm tired of life, tired of religion, and especially of Seventh-day Adventists, the whole shootin' shebang of 'em. From now on I am going to do whatever I want to do. I'm even tired of God!"

That last statement gave Maria second thoughts about calling security. She decided that this boy needed something else. "Sit down," she said. "Let's talk." He complied.

"Well, now, you have a problem," she said. "Tell me your name so we can talk."

"David."

"Mine's Maria. Now tell me, David, why are you tired of God?"

"I've had too much of Him. He keeps lettin' me down. He answers everyone else's prayers, but not mine. I don't want anything more to do with Him." The lines on David's face tightened, and his cheeks flushed; but he held on to himself, gripping the arm of his chair.

"Do you know what I do when someone has let me down?" Maria asked.

"What?"

"First I go talk to that person. Communication usually smooths the ruffled waters, and we both feel better."

David hesitated. "Then, you're telling me to pray."

"If you want to call it that. I call it communication."

"I've already tried that. It didn't work."

"Would you like to try it again?" Maria stood up. "Come with me." She reached out her hand and he took it, following her into the faculty lounge. Maria sat down. "You can kneel if you want to while I pray." He knelt in front of her, holding both her hands. She prayed a short prayer, then said, "Now you tell God just what you told me."

"God," David said, "You've been letting me down. You answer other people's prayers, but never mine. Remember how I asked You to make my girlfriend love me, and the next day she accepted a date with another guy? Is that fair? There are dozens of things I've asked You for, but You never seem to hear my prayers. Not even once did You answer me. You are nasty, mean, and I want You to get off my back!"

Then Maria prayed again, "Jesus, forgive David his bitterness. Take it out of his life and tell him how much You love him. Come close to him. Break this stubborn attitude." By the time Maria said Amen, David was crying and squeezing her hands.

They got up and David looked at Maria through his tears—such a different look from the one he had given her before. "Thank you, Maria," he whispered.

However, Maria could see that the struggle wasn't over yet. "Come, sit down and tell me about it," she said. David sat in a chair facing her.

"I thought I'd never want to hear the name of Jesus again," he said, "but as you prayed I felt His love around me, and now I know I was wrong. Jesus *does* love me. The girl I wanted is too good a Christian for me at this stage, but maybe I can change with His help. I know Jesus will work things out for me for what's best. I want to give my heart to Him right now. Will you pray for me every day?"

"Of course I will," Maria said with a smile. "I'm so glad you found Jesus again. He is your best Friend, you know."

"I know. Maria, did you know my parents are outside in the car with all my things packed? They're waiting to take me home. That's why I'm dressed this way. They came because I called them and told them I wouldn't stay at this school another day, and if they didn't come get me, I'd run away. It about broke Mother's heart. She had counted on my finding Christ in this college. I've hurt her so much in the past couple years. I'm going out there and tell her that I'm sorry and that I've found Jesus again and now things will be different."

"They'll be so happy," Maria murmured.

"I'll never forget you, Maria," he said as he stood to leave.

"Never forget me?" Maria asked. "All right, David, you can remember me, but there's Someone more important for you to remember, and that's Jesus."

"I will. I promise I will remember Jesus." David flashed a smile at Maria as he sprinted toward the door. Just before he went out, he turned and looked at her again. "Thanks for not calling security," he said, grinning at her.

"I called Jesus instead. That's always the best plan."

David nodded and ran out the door.

Maria, As She Is Now

One end of a far-reaching rainbow begins in Maria's heart. Perhaps this is because she has often watered her seeds of love and sunshine for others with her own tears. From her home at Andrews University it streams out across the North American continent.

Sometimes the other end of the rainbow can be found at camp meetings in Florida, Indiana, Michigan, or Canada when she addresses large audiences. Other times it can be found at youth rallies in New York or California. By air Maria follows her rainbow to deliver lectures at Adelphian Academy in Michigan or Parkview Adventist Academy in Canada. She has preached in many English and Spanish churches.

Maria often travels by train to her speaking engagements, rather than by plane, because the train is slower. The passengers usually welcome conversation as a diversion far more than the movie-watchers on a fast, one-martini flight. Maria always prays that these conversations will lead to conversion.

Whenever Maria travels, she always "happens" to have religious booklets with her, which she uses for tips as well as to reinforce her religious conversations. Maria always finds her pot of gold long before she reaches the end of her rainbow. People reward her with appreciative remarks like, "You are bringing sunshine to people," or "God bless you. If I don't see you again, I'll see you in heaven."

Maria has retired from work, but she will never retire from her prayer, "Give me one more soul, Lord, just one more soul." She lives near Andrews University in a beautifully landscaped apartment complex. Henrique, now a deeply devoted Seventh-day Adventist, and his wife, Carmen, live nearby. Their daughter, Helen, lives with her husband and two daughters at Andrews University, where Helen teaches Spanish at Andrews Academy while John is earning a master's degree in business. Dulcita and Gary also, with their two sons, live at Andrews, where Dulcita teaches. They are all one happy family and get together often, most recently for Jennie's fifth birthday dinner (Helen's daughter).

Because Maria is continually looking for one more soul, there is already a backlog of stories that should have been squeezed into these pages. There is the girl on a train whose screaming baby she quieted and then helped spiritually, her two nieces she rescued from joining a counterfeit tongues movement, the devil-possessed woman she prayed for and talked out of suicide, the spiritually confused student on the plane she recruited to come to Andrews, a discouraged Adventist who was working on his car engine on Sabbath that she brought close to the Lord again, a man who was smoking and drinking but who promised her he would pray once a day and read just a little from his Bible—and then was persuaded when he read the Beatitudes, and oh, so many more experiences!

Maria's story will never be finished until the remainder is told in Heaven.